Fangs for the Memories

Bethany House Books by

Bill Myers

Journeys to Fayrah

CHILDREN'S ALLEGORICAL SERIES

The Portal
The Experiment
The Whirlwind
The Tablet

Bloodhounds, Inc.

CHILDREN'S MYSTERY SERIES

The Ghost of KRZY
The Mystery of the Invisible Knight
Phantom of the Haunted Church
Invasion of the UFOs
Fangs for the Memories

Nonfiction

The Dark Side of the Supernatural
Hot Topics, Tough Questions

99B

5

BloodHounds, Inc.

Fangs for the Memories

Bill Myers

with David Wimbish

BETHANY HOUSE PUBLISHERS
MINNEAPOLIS, MINNESOTA 55438

Fangs for the Memories

Cover illustration by Joe Nordstrom
Cover design by the Lookout Design Group

Published by Bethany House Publishers
A Ministry of Bethany Fellowship International
11400 Hampshire Avenue South
Minneapolis, Minnesota 55438
www.bethanyhouse.com

Printed in the United States of America by
Bethany Press International, Minneapolis, Minnesota 55438

Library of Congress Cataloging-in-Publication Data

Myers, Bill, 1953–
Fangs for the memories / by Bill Myers.
p. cm. — (Bloodhounds, Inc. ; 5)
SUMMARY: When a vampire torments the people of their town, Sean and his sister Melissa use their detective skills and depend on the help of God to deal with the problem.
ISBN 1-55661-489-6
[1. Vampires Fiction. 2. Brothers and sisters Fiction. 3. Christian life Fiction. 4. Mystery and detective stories.] I. Title.
II. Series: Myers, Bill, 1953– Bloodhounds, Inc. ; 5.
PZ7.M98234 Fan 1999
[Fic]—dc21 99-6408
CIP

To Robert Elmer—

Another writer with a heart
dedicated to helping the young.

BILL MYERS is a youth worker and creative writer and film director who co-created the "McGee and Me!" book and video series and whose work has received over forty national and international awards. His many youth books include THE INCREDIBLE WORLDS OF WALLY MCDOOGLE, JOURNEYS TO FAYRAH, as well as his teen books, *Hot Topics, Tough Questions* and *Forbidden Doors.*

Contents

"The one who is in you is greater than the one who is in the world."

1 John 4:4

1

The Case Begins

FRIDAY, 20:53 PDST

Mrs. Hildagard Tubbs was in an unusually good mood. And Mrs. Tubbs was hardly ever in a good mood. In fact, she was usually your basic triple-A, award-winning *grouch*.

But not tonight. Tonight, her all-time favorite movie was on TV. That famous tearjerker of a love story *I Thought You Were Beautiful Until I Found My Glasses*. Even though she'd seen it nineteen times, she never got tired of it. She always pictured herself in the role of Juliet, the beautiful but tragic nurse who falls in love with some guy who gets run over by a bus and is unconscious for thirteen and a half years.

Mrs. Tubbs had been waiting all day for the movie to start. She'd already turned off the lights downstairs, and now she was upstairs getting ready for bed. As soon as the opening credits began, she flipped off the lights, hopped on the bed, and got ready to cry her eyes out.

She wore her prettiest gown, a gallon and a half of perfume, and of course, her fuzzy-wuzzy bunny slippers. On the bed beside her were three boxes of tissues for the usual eye wiping and nose blowing. On the other side was a tin of chocolates and a half gallon of Chewy-Gooey Caramel Swirl ice cream. And curled up at her feet was her beloved Precious, purring away.

Yes, sir, the evening was going to be great!

Mrs. Tubbs grabbed a tissue and got ready. The bus accident was only seven minutes into the movie, and that always opened the floodgates of tears. She popped a chocolate into her mouth and waited. But it had been a long day, and her eyes began to grow heavy. Very heavy. She fought to keep them open, but it was a losing battle.

The next thing she knew, she was no longer Hildagard Tubbs, but the young and beautiful Juliet, screaming in terror as the handsome doctor was hit by the bus and went flying into the air. She raced toward him.

"Oh, Dr. Handsome," she murmured in her sleep. "I hope that mean old bus didn't mess up your handsome face! But I love you even if it did."

Dr. Handsome came to, opened his unbelievably

handsome eyes, and spoke something.

She leaned closer to hear. "What was that?" she asked. "What did you say, my love?"

"Hissss . . . meowwwwrrr!"

"I'm sorry. I don't think I got that."

"Hissssss!"

"Dr. Handsome. You sound like . . . like a pussycat!"

"Meeoowwr! Hissssss!"

Mrs. Tubbs startled awake. In the flickering light of the TV, she saw Precious standing on her bed, staring out the window with his back arched. Every hair on his body stuck straight up . . . until he leaped off the bed and scrambled underneath it. That's when Mrs. Tubbs spun toward the window.

She wished she hadn't. Because there, hovering just outside, was a giant bat! She could see the light shining in its huge eyes and hear the soft whirring of its wings as they beat the air.

Mrs. Tubbs gasped and rubbed her eyes.

The good news was the bat was gone. The bad news was there was now a man in its place. And the worst news was he looked exactly like a vampire. Actually, there was one piece of news that was even worse than that worst. . . .

He was trying to climb in through her window!

In a panic, Mrs. Tubbs pinched herself to see if she was still dreaming.

"Ouch!" No—she was definitely awake.

She watched in horror as he opened the window and climbed inside. It was definitely a vampire, complete with long, sharp fangs and a black cape flowing behind him.

He started toward her.

Mrs. Tubbs tried to breathe, but she couldn't catch her breath.

Suddenly the vampire stopped. His cape had caught on the edge of the window. He tugged and tugged and then tugged some more until it finally gave way with a rip.

Mrs. Tubbs wanted to run, but it's hard to run when you're paralyzed with fear.

The vampire continued toward her. One step, two steps, and then . . .

WOAH!

. . . he stepped in the ice cream, which had melted on the floor. His feet flew out from under him and . . .

THUMP!

. . . he landed hard on his rear.

But he was only there for a second. He quickly leaped back to his feet and continued his approach. Closer and closer he came until he finally reached her side. Then he bent over, his teeth flashing in the darkness.

Suddenly Mrs. Tubbs had a great idea. Maybe now would be a good time to start screaming for her life.

SATURDAY, 04:12 PDST

Sean Hunter pulled the pillow over his head, trying to drown out the noise. But it was no use.

EEEAAAGGGHH!

He opened one eye.

EEEAAAGGGHH!

He opened the other eye.

EEEAAAGGGHH!

"Stupid alarm clock," he mumbled. He reached out in the darkness and hit the Snooze button.

EEEAAAGGGHH!

It was still going. He swatted at the clock, missed it, and sent the nearby lamp tumbling to the floor.

EEEAAAGGGHH!

His next swing hit its target, and he snuggled back

down into his comfortable, warm bed. All he needed was another ten minutes of sleep. He'd still be able to make it to school in time if he skipped breakfast and—

EEEAAAGGGHH!

He sat up in bed. He'd hit the Snooze button, he was sure of it. Wait a minute. His alarm had never sounded like that before. Wait another minute. It was Saturday! There was no school on Saturday.

"Sean! Sean!" His sister, Melissa, began banging on the door. "Sean! Get up! Somebody's in trouble!"

"Hold on . . ." he shouted, "I'm coming!"

EEEAAAGGGHH!

He threw off the covers and ran for the door. At least, that's what he wanted to do. But somehow one foot got tangled in his blanket while the other landed on the fallen lamp. So instead of running to the door, Sean went crashing to the . . .

Ker-Whump!

. . . floor.

He struggled to sit up. Oh no, he couldn't see! Not a thing! He must have fallen so hard that he went blind or . . . He put his hands up to his head. Whew, it was just the lampshade stuck on his head. No problem . . . except for the part where he couldn't get it off.

"Sean!" Melissa cried. "Are you up?"

"I'm coming! I'm coming!"

He staggered to his feet, trying to untangle himself from his blanket, trying to get the shade off his head, when . . .

BAMB!

. . . he ran into the wall. And then . . .

BAMB!

. . . he ran into the other wall.

And then, just when it looked like he was starting to run out of walls to *bamb* into, Melissa threw open the door with Slobs, their faithful bloodhound, right behind.

"Will you quit clowning around!" she shouted. "Someone needs our help!"

"I know, I—"

BAMB!

He'd found another wall.

"Sean, what are you doing?"

He turned to the voice. Unfortunately, with his blanket wrapped around him and the lampshade stuck over his head, he looked like some type of invader from another world.

"Rowfff! Rowfff! Rowfff!" Good ol' Slobs. She wasn't about to let some monster from another world threaten her family! She leaped at Sean, hitting him square in the chest with all of her 102 pounds and . . .

"AUGH!"
THUMP!

Once again, Sean was on the floor.

"Grrrrrrr!" Slobs was on top of him now, doing her best to sound vicious and threatening.

"Slobs! It's me! It's Sean!"

The dog stopped growling, sat back, and cocked her head to one side. At last Sean managed to pull the lampshade off his head. "See! It's only me!"

Slobs was all over him again, this time covering him with slobbery wet kisses—and drool, lots and lots of drool.

"Oh gross!" Sean yelled. "I liked it better when you were attacking me!"

EEEAAAGGGHH!

"What *is* that noise?" he asked.

"Someone's screaming," Melissa answered. "It's coming from Mrs. Tubbs' house."

Sean groaned. "Oh no, what'd we do this time?" It seems Mrs. Tubbs was always upset about something, and it always had to do with them. Actually, it always had to do with Slobs, who loved chasing her big, fluffy cat, Precious.

EEEAAAGGGHH!

"She sounds pretty scared!" Melissa shouted. "We'd better hurry."

Sean nodded, untangled himself from the blanket, and ran out the door. Melissa and Slobs were right behind.

2

Vampires Are a Pain in the Neck

SATURDAY, 04:30 PDST

By the time Sean and Melissa reached Mrs. Tubbs, she had stopped screaming. She was in her front yard, still wearing her nightgown and wringing her hands, as Dad and several other neighbors tried to calm her down.

"It was horrible!" she cried. "He came in through the window. Scared me to death!"

"Who, Mrs. Tubbs?" asked a neighbor. "Did you get a good look at him? What did he look like?"

"I'll never forget. He was horrible! I think it was a vam . . . a vam . . ." She buried her face in her hands and began to sob.

"A van?" someone asked.

"Maybe she means he was a van driver?" another suggested.

"I think she said, 'ven,' " someone else chimed in. "I'll bet she was attacked by a ventriloquist! I've never trusted those people."

"No . . . no . . ." sobbed Mrs. Tubbs. "A vam . . ." But she couldn't get out the word.

"I tink she vas attack-ed by a vamily," said Mr. Wyss, the old next-door neighbor from Germany.

"No! No! No!" shouted Mrs. Tubbs, who was becoming frustrated at all the wrong guesses. "It was a vampire!"

"A vampire!" everyone cried.

"That's right! A vampire! He flew in my window . . . and I think he bit me on the neck, and now I'm probably going to turn into a vampire, too!" She went back to her sobbing.

"A vampire?" Dad repeated. "Mrs. Tubbs, I know you're frightened. But really . . . you know there's no such thing as a vampire. Maybe you just had a bad dream."

"I did not! He came in my window right after Dr. Handsome got run over by that bus, and . . ."

"Dr. Handsome got run ofer by a bus?" Mr. Wyss asked. He glanced at the others and pointed to his head, making little circular motions with his finger.

Mrs. Tubbs spotted him and cried, "I am not crazy! There he was, lying on the street, and the next thing I knew, there was this vampire . . . with flashing fangs, and a long black cape, and . . ."

Melissa tapped her brother on the shoulder. "What if Mrs. Tubbs is telling the truth?" she whispered. "What if she really was attacked by a vampire?"

"Don't be silly," Sean scoffed. "You heard Dad. There's no such thing as a vampire."

"I wouldn't be too sure!" an electronic voice squawked—a voice that seemed to be coming straight from Sean's wrist.

Sean glanced down to his digital wristwatch and whispered, "Shh, Jeremiah, they'll hear you."

The little leprechaun-like creature looked up from Sean's watch and stuck his tongue out as his face changed from green to blue to red and back to green. "Are you ashamed of me?" he asked.

"Of course not. But you know what happens when people see you. You scare them!"

"*I* scare *them*!" the little guy giggled. "Now, that's a house of a different color. A vampire's on the loose and *I* scare them?"

Now, Jeremiah wasn't exactly a real person . . . but you couldn't tell him that. No, sir. Jeremiah—which stood for *J*ohnson *E*lectronic *R*eductive *E*ntity *M*emory *I*nductive *A*ssembly *H*ousing—had been invented by Sean and Melissa's brilliant scientist friend, Doc. As an electronic character, you never knew where Jeremiah would show up next—on digital watches, TV sets, computer games. You name it, if it had electricity, he could go to it. But it seemed every time the little fellow showed up, people panicked. So the poor guy usually had to stay hidden from everybody except Sean, Melissa, and Doc.

"There's no such thing as a vampire," Sean whispered back to him.

"Oh no?" Jeremiah challenged. "Looks to me like Mrs. Tubbs is already turning into one."

Sean looked over and gasped. In the dim light of early morning, Mrs. Tubbs really did look . . . well . . . ghastly. And that was being polite. Her thin white hair was pointed in twenty-seven different directions. A thick black liquid oozed from the corner of her eyes and ran down her face. And her lips were bright red!

"Yikes!" Melissa whispered. "She does look like a vampire!"

Seeing them stare, Mrs. Tubbs reached for her face and immediately cried out, "Oh my goodness!" Suddenly she remembered all that makeup she'd put on her face as she made believe she was the beautiful nurse in the movie. And now all that makeup was smeared all over her face. "I must look terrible!"

"Nonsense!" Dad said. "You don't look . . . well, that

is to say . . . you don't look too bad."

Sean and Melissa knew Dad was one of the best men in Midvale, and certainly one of the nicest. But he was a terrible liar, and they could see Mrs. Tubbs wasn't buying it for a second.

"Not that bad?" she cried. "With my makeup all smeared and mascara running down my face? I look awful!"

"When she's left, she's left," Jeremiah quipped. (Of course, he meant, "When she's right, she's right," but Jeremiah always got a little confused when it came to using sayings—ever since he'd been trapped in that computer of a Chinese fortune cookie factory for the whole night.)

"I know none of you believe me," Mrs. Tubbs said, "but I'm not crazy, and I know what I saw. Maybe the police will take me seriously."

She turned on her heels and strode back to her house. As she reached her front door, she looked back over her shoulder and called to Sean, "You kids still got that detective agency? What do you call it? Hotdogs, Incorporated?"

"*Bloodhounds*, Incorporated," Melissa corrected.

"Whatever. I'll make you a deal. You catch this vampire, and I'll pay you fifty dollars."

"Fifty dollars!" Sean cried.

"All right. Make it a hundred."

"A hundred dollars?" Sean practically choked. "You've got yourself a deal."

"Are you crazy?" Melissa warned. "We're talking real, bloodsucking vamp—"

"We'll be right over," Sean shouted back to Mrs. Tubbs. "Just give us a few minutes."

Melissa was right behind her brother as he rushed around his room, gathering up the equipment they needed to begin their investigation. "Are you really sure you want to get involved with vampires?" she asked. "I mean, crooks are one thing . . . but monsters. . . ?"

"I don't believe in monsters," Sean answered as he threw a can of fingerprint dusting powder into his duffel bag. Unfortunately, he threw it a bit too hard. It bounced out of the bag and landed on the floor . . . not, of course, without losing its lid and spilling white powder all over the carpet.

"Oh man," Sean groaned. "This stuff is expensive. Help me get it up."

Unfortunately, Slobs got there first. Intrigued by the smell, she took a deep sniff . . .

SNZXXXXXX!

. . . and the powder disappeared up her nose.

The big dog took a step back and cocked her head to one side. Then to the other. Next, her eyes crossed and began to water. Finally she opened her mouth wide.

"AH . . . AH . . . AH . . ."

"Look out!" Melissa yelled. "She's gonna blow!"

"AH . . . CHOOOOO!"

A cloud of powder spewed out of Slobs' nose.

"AH . . . CHOOOOO!"

And again.

"What should we do?" Melissa cried.

"I . . . don't know," Sean shouted.

"AH . . . CHOOOOO!"
"AH . . . CHOOOOO!"

The big dog began running in circles, sneezing and spouting out fingerprint powder like an old-fashioned steam engine.

"Maybe we should give her some water," Melissa yelled.

"Good idea!"

Sean ran downstairs to the kitchen, filled her bowl with water, and raced back up. Slobs drank like there was no tomorrow. That seemed to do the trick. She sneezed once more, but there was no explosion of powder this time. Then with an exhausted sigh, she flopped down on the floor to do what she did best . . . drool.

Sean patted her head. "You okay, girl?"

She looked up, licked her chops, and belched. Yes, sir, everything was back to normal. Or at least as normal as it ever got in the Hunter home.

Sean bent down and picked up the empty can of powder. "Looks like we're going to have to buy some more of this pretty soon," he said as he placed it in the duffel bag. "But that's okay. With the money Mrs. Tubbs is paying us, we can buy all sorts of fingerprint powder. And lots of other cool stuff, too."

Melissa shrugged. "Like what?"

"Like, well . . . I . . . uh . . . I'm not sure. But we'll be able to buy a lot of it!"

"I don't know," Melissa said. "I'm kinda worried."

"Can't turn chicken on me now," Sean said as he tossed a magnifying glass into the duffel bag. "We're in this together. Bloodhounds, Incorporated. That means we're partners, and just because you're getting cold feet doesn't mean we—" Sean stopped midsentence when he saw Dad standing in the doorway. "Oh . . . hi, Dad."

"Hi, guys. Having a little business disagreement?"

"Not really," Sean said. "I was just explaining to Misty here that Mrs. Tubbs probably had a bad dream. That's it. Case closed."

Dad nodded. "Probably. But if it was only a dream, how are you going to collect a hundred dollars for catching the vampire?"

"Yeah," Melissa agreed. "How are we gonna do that?"

"No sweat."

Both looked at him, waiting for an answer.

"Well . . . we just . . . uh . . . that is to say . . . uh . . ."

"That's what I thought," Melissa sighed. Then turning to Dad, she asked, "Are you really sure there's no such thing as a vampire?"

Her father nodded. "If we're talking about people who've died and go around drinking other people's blood to stay alive—there's absolutely no such thing."

"How can you be so sure?"

"We've talked about this before. God says that when people die, they go directly to Him to face judgment. No hanging around as ghosts or vampires or whatever."

Melissa nodded but didn't seem entirely convinced.

"Besides," he continued, "even if they did exist, you wouldn't have to worry."

"Why's that?" Melissa asked.

Dad broke into a smile and quoted one of his favorite

Bible verses. " 'The one who is in you is greater than the one who is in the world.' You've got God on your side, remember?"

With a heavy sigh, Melissa sat down on the edge of her brother's bed.

"What's wrong, sweetheart?"

"I believe the Bible, Dad. Really. It's just that . . ." She let her voice trail off.

"It's just what, honey?"

"Well, ever since Mom died . . ." She looked away, unable to continue.

Dad understood and crossed the room to sit beside her. It had been less than a year since Melissa and Sean's Mom had lost her fight against cancer. How they all missed her warm smile, her gentle laughter, and her understanding touch. As a family, they had prayed for her to get well. But she had died anyway. And now there was an ache in all of their hearts that they thought would never go away.

When Dad spoke, his voice was thick with emotion. "Go ahead, honey. Ever since Mom died, what?"

"Well, sometimes I have trouble believing, you know, that God is going to take care of us."

Dad looked down at his hands and nodded. Finally he spoke. "I don't know why your mother died. Believe me, I miss her as much as you guys do. But I know this: I know she's in heaven, and I know that we're going to see her again someday."

Melissa sighed. "Yeah . . . I just don't know why she had to go so soon."

Dad pulled her closer. "Neither do I, honey. Neither do I." Then, after a deep breath, he continued. "But I know God can be trusted. In whatever situation you find yourself, He'll be there for you. He'll always be there."

"Even when it comes to tracking down make-believe vampires?" Sean asked from across the room.

Dad smiled. "Even when it comes to tracking down make-believe vampires."

"Then what are we waiting for?" Sean said as he grabbed the duffel bag and headed for the door. "We don't want to keep Mrs. Tubbs and her hundred dollars waiting. Let's go!"

Melissa sighed one last time. Big brothers can be such a pain sometimes. But he was right; they had agreed to help. And Dad was right, too; God could be trusted. At least that's what she hoped. So, rising from the bed, she gave Dad a quick kiss on the cheek and followed her brother out the door to whatever fate awaited them. . . .

3

Hic . . . Hic . . . Hiccups

SATURDAY, 05:45 PDST

Mrs. Tubbs' bedroom was a mess.

Drawers were half open with clothes hanging out. Books and papers were scattered about. Small chocolate candies were strewn all over the floor.

"Wow," Sean said, "did the vampire do all of this?"

"Uh . . . no, not really," said Mrs. Tubbs, a little embarrassed. "It usually looks this way. Except for the candy, of course. You see, I fell asleep while I was—"

"Wait a minute. What's this?" Sean interrupted. On the floor beside Mrs. Tubbs' bed was a gooey, sticky mess of . . . something.

Before the kids had a chance to examine it, Slobs leaped on top of it and began licking away with all of her might.

"Slobs, stop!" Melissa shouted. "You're eating the evidence!"

"Oh, I'm sorry," Mrs. Tubbs said. "That's not really evidence. As I was saying, I must have fallen asleep while I was eating. That's just my melted ice cream."

Soon Slobs had licked the floor clean. She looked up with a satisfied smile, smacked her chops, and burped. She was a great burper.

For the next several minutes, Sean and Melissa carefully checked out Mrs. Tubbs' bedroom for clues. Well, actually, Sean checked for clues. Melissa, being a neat freak, spent the time going around straightening up everything. Because if there was one thing she hated, it was a mess. She folded clothes and put them back in the drawers. She stacked papers neatly, put books back on shelves, and pretty much made the room look like hers—spotless.

Meanwhile, Sean's investigation turned up nothing. Of course, he didn't want Mrs. Tubbs to know that, so in his best official detective voice, he said, "We're going to go home and analyze the clues. We'll be back later to ask you some more questions."

He turned to Melissa. "Are you ready to go?"

"Almost. Just let me straighten this curtain here, and . . . wait a minute, what's this?" She pulled out a piece of torn black cloth caught on the corner of the windowsill.

Sean moved closer to look.

"That's part of his cape!" Mrs. Tubbs cried. "He caught his cape on the windowsill when he came through the window!"

Sean and Melissa turned and looked at each other, their eyes widening in wonder.

SATURDAY, 09:16 PDST

"Maybe she's not home," Sean said.

The two of them stood on Doc's front porch as Melissa pushed the doorbell again. But it made no sound. The reason was simple: Doc was deaf. So instead of chimes or a buzzer, the woman had a special vibrator built into her watch so she could feel whenever anyone pushed the doorbell.

Impressive? Yes. But pretty normal for the way Doc did things. Besides being an incredible inventor, Doc was a brilliant scientist who'd helped the kids solve their toughest cases. Now Sean and Melissa were hoping she'd have time to analyze the cloth, to see if it held any clues about who—or what—had been in Mrs. Tubbs' bedroom.

"I think I hear someone coming," Sean said.

Sure enough, the front door swung open with an eerie

CREAK. But instead of Doc, the kids came face-to-face with a big guy in overalls.

"Oh hi," he said. "I didn't hear you ring the bell. I was just going out to my truck for a wrench. Somethin' I can do for you?"

"Who are you?" Melissa asked. "And where's Doc?"

The man pointed at his name tag. "The name's Bruce, and I'm here to fix the washing machine."

"We're Doc's friends," Sean said, "and we need to talk to her."

"Yeah, it's real important," Melissa added.

Bruce opened the door wider. "Come on in," he said. "But good luck getting her attention. She's all tied up with some new invention. Not sure what it is, but she's really into it."

"Oh," said Melissa, "so that's why she called a repairman. Normally she'd fix something like a washer herself."

"Unless, of course, she didn't want it blowing up." Sean smirked. (Although Doc was a great inventor, it usually took her two or three times until she got things right.)

"She's in the lab," Bruce said, pointing upstairs toward the attic. "I better get back to work."

The kids found Doc in the lab, bent over her workbench. Lots of diagrams and drawings were spread all over the place. When she finally looked up to see them, she simply nodded.

"Hey, Doc," Sean said, making sure she saw his lips so she could read them. "What are you working on?"

It's called the Domesticus IV Household Servant, she signed with her hands.

"Cool!" said Sean. "But why the number four?"

Because the first three had a few bugs in them.

"Right," Sean chuckled, "so what else is new?"

Doc ignored him and signed, *When he's perfected, he'll cook, clean, do laundry—everything that needs to be done around the house. Let me show you.*

She clicked a button, and a huge, scary robot clanked into the room. In his iron claw he carried a glass of lemonade.

Doc took the lemonade and offered the kids a sip.

Melissa shook her head. "That's pretty impressive. But isn't he kind of . . . scary looking?"

"I'll say," Sean agreed. "Looks like a heavy-metal version of Frankenstein."

Doc sighed and signed, *You're right. I'll have to work on that. But he's really as gentle as a lamb.*

Suddenly Melissa remembered why they'd come. "Sean, show her what we have."

"Oh, right."

Sean reached into his pocket and pulled out a plastic bag containing the torn piece of black cloth. "We were wondering if you could analyze this for us," he said. "Someone thinks it was part of a vampire's cape and—"

"Vampire? Vampire?"

The voice came from Doc's computer monitor. Sean and Melissa turned to see colors swirling through static until Jeremiah's form finally appeared. The little guy was upset . . . big-time.

"I told you—stay away from the vampire," his little voice squeaked. "It will hurt you! It will drink your blood! It will drink my blood!"

"Jeremiah," Melissa scorned. "You don't *have* blood!"

Suddenly he disappeared from the monitor and was back in Sean's wristwatch. "That doesn't matter," he said. "Never look a gift house in the mouth, because he might have vampire teeth that can . . . *hic* . . . sure . . . *hic* . . . ruin your . . . *hic* . . . day!"

"Jeremiah!" Melissa cried. "What's wrong with you?"

"Hic," Jeremiah answered. "I'm . . . afrai . . . *hic* . . . afrai . . . *hic* . . . scared of vampires!"

"He's so scared, he has the hiccups!" Sean exclaimed.

"Hic!" Jeremiah agreed.

"Hey, stop it!" Bruce yelled from downstairs.

"Hic!"

"Cut it out!" The repairman sounded pretty angry.

Sean and Melissa glanced at each other, then headed down the steps to investigate. They found the big man in the kitchen, soaking wet and looking for a towel. Water dripped from his eyes, his ears, and his nose, and his sneakers squished as he walked.

"What happened to you?" Melissa asked.

"I don't know. Something's wrong with the washing machine. It's acting crazy!"

"Hic!" Jeremiah hiccuped from Sean's watch, and a geyser of water flew up out of the washing machine and . . .

Splash!

. . . landed on the floor.

Jeremiah hiccuped again and . . .

Splash!

. . . more water.

Sean and Melissa exchanged looks. Neither knew what was happening, but they figured it had something to do with their little pal's hiccups. Somehow he had tapped into the washing machine's electrical circuit. Now every time he hiccuped, so did the washing machine.

"Hic!"

Splash!

Bruce grabbed a towel and leaned over the kitchen sink to dry his bald head. He didn't notice that the end of the towel was hanging in the garbage disposal until . . .

"Hic!"

WHIRRRRRRR!

The garbage disposal roared to life, grabbing the towel and pulling Bruce facedown into the sink.

BONK!

"OW!" he yelled, then raised back up and staggered across the kitchen.

"Hic!"

K-SMACK!

K-SMACK!

"EEYOW!"

Now the toaster had gotten into the act, firing pieces of whole wheat toast into his back.

"What are we gonna do?" Melissa cried.

"I don't know!" Sean yelled. "How do you cure hiccups?"

"Put a paper bag over his head?" Melissa shouted.

"Good idea!" Sean opened the pantry door and rummaged around for a paper sack.

"Hic!"

BZZZZZZZZZ!

Now the mixer went into action with the cake dough Domesticus IV had been using.

SPLAT! PLAP! THWACK!

. . . sending gobs of the gooey goop across the room, directly into Bruce's face.

"Augh . . ." he cried as he staggered blindly around the room.

"I got a bag!" Sean shouted as he pulled one from the pantry. He opened it and tried to get it over Bruce's head, but the man was moving too much and the bag was too small.

"Not his head!" Melissa shouted. She pointed to Sean's wristwatch. "*His* head!"

"Oh . . . right."

Sean stuck his left hand in the bag and then wrapped it shut.

"Hey! What are you doing?" Jeremiah's voice was muffled inside the sack.

"I'm curing your hiccups!" Sean yelled.

"Well . . . it . . . *hic!* . . ."

ZING . . . ZING . . . ZING . . .

The ice maker shot a volley of ice cubes across the room.

"*. . .* isn't working . . . *hic!*"

ZING . . . ZING . . . ZING . . .

Another round of cubes.

"Woof! Woof!" Slobs jumped into the air, trying to catch one of the ice cubes in her mouth. When she came down, she slipped on the cake batter and went sliding . . . right into Bruce, which sent him tumbling, head over heels, to the ground . . . with Slobs landing on top.

"Oaff!"

That's when she tasted the batter on his face and suddenly began licking it off as fast as she could. And as we all know, with bloodhound licks comes bloodhound drool. . . .

"Get her (*choke choke*) off!" Bruce cried.

"Slobs!"

"Get her (*gag gag*) off!"

"SLOBS!"

The frightened repairman scrambled to his feet. "I gotta get outa here!" he cried. "I gotta get out!" He ran for the front door, but before he could get there . . .

"Hic!"

Another electronic burp from Jeremiah brought Doc's VCR to life . . .

K-Pow!

. . . causing a video tape to fly out of the machine and smash into Bruce's rear.

"Eeeeyow!" He grabbed his backside and raced out the door.

Melissa ran after him. "Bruce! Come back!"

"No way!" he shouted.

"But . . . what about the washing machine?"

"She can fix it herself!" he shouted over his shoulder. "It's not safe in that hou—!"

"Look out!" Melissa yelled. "Watch where you're—"

K-RRAASSHH!

Too late! Bruce had run straight into three kids on their bikes—KC, Spalding, and Bear. KC was the toughest girl in town (even though she was knee-high to a Munchkin). Spalding was the richest kid in town. And Bear was . . . well, he was just Bear.

All three hit Bruce about the same time, which sent him tumbling down the street, while they went flying off their bikes, landing facedown in Doc's flower bed.

"Yeaghhhh!"

"Sppiffff!"

"Thttttttt!"

All three sat up, spitting out mouthfuls of dirt. Actually, it was more like mud, since it had been swished around pretty good in their mouths first.

The good news was no one was hurt . . . not even Bruce. In fact, he was already on his feet, running back down the street for his life.

KC was almost in as big a hurry. "Quick!" she shouted to the other two, who were still spitting mini mud pies out of their mouths. "We can't waste time here. Get your bikes and let's get going."

"What's the hurry?" Sean asked as he approached.

"We're going to the police!"

"The police?" Melissa said. "Why?"

"To tell them about the vampire!"

"Vampire?" Sean threw a nervous glance at Melissa. "What vampire are you talking about?"

"The one that moved into the old Zanker house," KC answered.

"What?!" Sean and Melissa cried together.

"That is correct," Spalding nodded. "As a matter of fact, we have actually seen his coffin through the window."

"No way!" Sean scoffed.

"Oh yeah, big way," KC answered.

Sean shook his head. "You did not see any vampire's coffin."

"Sure did," little KC insisted. "We'd take you there right now, but you're probably too chicken to go up and look in the window."

"Chicken?" Sean forced a nervous laugh. "We're not chicken of anything." He turned to Melissa. "Are we, Misty?"

Melissa gave a nervous smile and an even more nervous cough. "No, uh . . . of course not."

"Oh yeah?" KC taunted.

"Yeah."

"Then come on!" KC ordered. "The police can wait. Right now I want to see how brave the great Sean Hunter is. But if you start clucking and laying eggs, don't blame me!"

4

City Under Attack

SATURDAY, 10:57 PDST

By the time the kids reached the old Zanker house, the bright, sunny morning had turned dark and eerie. Heavy black clouds had blown in from the west and covered the sun. Everything looked strangely dark and, even if Sean wouldn't admit it . . . scary.

The Zanker place was one of the oldest houses in Midvale—more than one hundred years old—and by far the spookiest. It looked like *The X-Files* meets *The Twilight Zone* (with a little *Buffy the Vampire Slayer* thrown in just to make things interesting).

One of the third-story windows had been broken for as long as anyone could remember. Some of the shutters were loose and banged whenever there was a breeze. Nobody had lived in the house since old man Zanker died over five years ago. Nobody was crazy enough to try.

Until now . . .

Now there was a strange sort of light glowing from inside. Sean took a deep breath and swallowed. But at the moment there was nothing left in his mouth to swallow. He glanced down at Slobs. The dog always helped bolster his courage, but at the moment she was whining softly with her tail between her legs.

So much for courage.

"What are you waiting for?" KC croaked. "Go on over there and take a look."

"I will," Sean said. "But first, I . . . uh, I need you to tell me exactly what you saw."

Spalding snickered and in his richest, snobbiest voice, said, "I do believe he is stalling on account of his fear."

"He is not afraid," Melissa said, coming to her brother's defense.

Sean turned to her. "I'm not?"

"No," she insisted. "We just need to make sure we've got all the facts before we begin the investigation."

KC rolled her eyes. "Yeah, right. Okay—we saw a moving van in front of the house, so we stopped to see what was going on. Naturally, we couldn't believe anybody wanted to live here."

"Naturally," Sean agreed.

"Well, the movers were carrying all kinds of weird furniture into the house. I mean, this stuff was really old—"

"And the last item they brought in," Spalding interrupted, "was a coffin."

"A coffin . . ." Sean's voice cracked slightly.

"That's right," said KC, "a coffin. Like the type a vampire would sleep in."

"Maybe it just looked like a coffin," Melissa suggested. "Maybe it was just a . . . a . . ." she turned to Sean for help.

"Yeah, that's right," Sean agreed, "maybe it was just a . . . a . . ."

"A what?" KC smirked.

Sean and Melissa looked at each other. Both were equally clueless.

"It *was* a coffin," KC repeated. "And just to make sure, I looked through that basement window over there and saw it again."

Sean followed her finger. "That window over there?"

"That's the one," KC said. "So go on over there and take a look for yourself . . . if you're not too chicken?"

"All right," Sean said. "I will." But even as his mouth spoke, his legs froze. Try as he might, he couldn't get them to move. What was wrong? It wasn't that he was afraid of a vampire, was it? After all, he didn't even believe in them.

Then again, they *had* found that piece of black cloth on Mrs. Tubbs' windowsill . . . and the old house did look awfully scary on this stormy afternoon.

"Well?" Bear asked. "You goin' or not?"

"Of course I'm going. I just have to . . . um . . . that is to say, I uh—"

Suddenly Slobs began barking.

"What is it, girl?" Melissa asked. "What's wrong?"

"There," Spalding pointed. "In that other window."

All eyes looked over to see the world's fattest cat jumping up into the living room window—the window just above the basement window. It sat inside there, as calm as you please, completely ignoring Slobs, almost as if it was taunting her.

It was more than the poor dog could handle. She was off like a bullet.

"Woof! Woof!"

"Slobs! No!" Melissa ran after her.

"Misty, wait!" Sean was right behind.

And the other three followed.

"Woof! Woof!"

Slobs arrived at the window, barking and growling for all she was worth . . . as the cat just sat there, doing his best to look bored.

"Woof! Grrrrr . . . Woof!"

The cat simply yawned.

Melissa grabbed Slobs around the neck. "It's okay, girl. Shh . . . it's okay. Come on!"

And that's when she saw it. Through the lower window. The one looking down into the basement.

"Sean . . ." she gasped.

"What?"

All she could do was point.

He followed her gaze until he saw it, too . . . through the window . . . down in the basement . . .

"The coffin!" he cried.

Everyone crowded together for a better look. It sat in a shadowy corner, and although the details weren't visible, the shape was unmistakable. It was a coffin, all right.

Sean's mind raced. Why would anyone have a coffin sitting in their basement? Unless, of course . . .

Crrreeeaaak . . .

Suddenly the house's big front door swung open.

Everybody spun around to it. Someone was standing in the shadows.

"Good morning," a craggy voice called. "Nice of you to stop by."

Sean opened his mouth to answer but wasn't sure if

he heard anything come out. It was hard to hear anything over his pounding heart, gasping breath, and knocking knees. It wasn't that he was afraid. It was just that . . . well, all right, he was terrified!

"Come over here," the voice said.

Sean and the others began backing away.

The vampire opened his door wider, beckoning them to come closer. "Please, I need—"

Sean didn't know who started running first. All he knew was that somehow all five kids—and one dog—were running for their lives.

"Wait. . . ! Come back!" the creature shouted. "Where are you going?"

But no one stuck around to answer.

"Dad! We're home!"

No response.

"Dad?" Melissa called again.

"He's at the radio station," Sean said. "This was on the table." He tossed a crumpled note at her. She ducked, then sighed and bent down to pick it up. (To have her brother hand it to her like a normal person would have been way too much to ask.)

Kids,

I'm at the station. Don't know when I'll be home. Herbie couldn't come in because he got his hand stuck in a bowling ball. Don't ask me how! I know you've been out all morning working on Mrs. Tubbs' case, but please don't forget to do your chores. There are some microwave dinners in the freezer.

Love, Dad

Melissa sighed again. As the owner and general manager of radio station KRZY, Dad had to spend a lot of time there—especially with a walking disaster area like Herbie working as his engineer. Just last month, Herbie had missed two days of work because he'd hit himself in the head with a tennis racquet. Before that he had swallowed a Ping-Pong ball. And now his hand was stuck in a bowling ball. Would the poor guy ever find a sport where he wouldn't hurt himself? Melissa had her doubts.

And so another Saturday found Dad working at the station instead of spending the day with his kids. Melissa was disappointed for a lot of reasons, but mostly because she had really wanted to talk to Dad again. She knew he didn't believe in vampires, but with all they were discovering, she needed to know more reasons why.

Sean was disappointed, too, but for something

entirely different. "Chores, shmores!" he muttered as he stomped into the living room. "Who's got time for housework when we're trying to catch a vampire?" He flipped on the TV and flopped down on the sofa.

"Hey! What's going on here?" he shouted. "Where are the cartoons?"

On the screen was a news program featuring investigative reporter Ricardo Ruelas. Ruelas was yelling into the microphone and swinging his arms around like crazy. But that didn't mean anything. Ruelas was always shouting into the microphone and swinging his arms around like crazy. He thought it made him look important.

"What's he yelling about this time?" Melissa asked as she came into the room.

"Who knows?" Sean yawned. "Remember how excited he got about the snail races last week at Miller's Pond?"

Melissa nodded. "Wanted to try to get them into next year's Olympics."

Sean sighed. "Oh well, might as well get on with those chores." He picked up the remote and was just about to click off the TV when he heard . . .

"That's right, ladies and gentlemen," Ruelas shouted, "I'm talking about vampires—right here in Midvale! Vicious vampire villains voraciously vexing village viewers—" Ruelas paused for a moment, obviously searching his mind for another word that started with *v*.

"Hey, look!" Melissa pointed at the TV. "It's Bruce!"

Sure enough, there was Bruce the repairman. But what on earth was he wearing? It looked like . . . it was . . . a straightjacket!

"And as if vampires aren't bad enough," Ruelas continued, "this local repairman has been hospitalized in shock after he was attacked by a vicious gang of haunted electrical appliances."

Ruelas thrust the microphone in Bruce's face. "Tell us what happened, sir!"

"Garb . . . garb . . . garbage disposal . . ." Bruce babbled.

"Go on," Ruelas said. "And then what?"

"Toas . . . toas . . . toaster . . ." Now Bruce was grimacing, trying to show where the toast had hit him in the back.

"It must have been terrifying!"

"Ow . . . ow . . . ow . . ." Now Bruce was motioning to his rear.

"Yes, well, thank you for that amazing firsthand account."

The camera closed in on Ruelas as two men in white coats appeared and carried Bruce away.

"Well, folks, there you have it. Vampires. Kitchen

appliances with a thirst for blood. It's clear that no one in Midvale is safe. Where will it all end? Must our entire town be destroyed by these monumentally monstrous monsters? And now . . . back to our regularly scheduled programming."

"Wow!" Melissa exclaimed. "Nothing like getting everybody all worked up."

"Ah, nobody pays any attention to him anyway," Sean said. "But he did give me a great idea."

"He did?" Melissa wasn't sure she wanted to hear it. One way or another, Sean's great ideas always wound up getting them into even greater trouble.

Sean nodded. "He sure did. You know how I said we don't have time to do our chores 'cause we're too busy chasing the vampire?"

"Uh . . . yeah. . . ?"

"Well . . . we don't *have* to do our chores."

"We don't?"

"No . . . we can get Domesticus IV to do them."

"Domesticus IV! Are you out of your—"

"Oh, come on," he said. "You worry too much. What could possibly go wrong?"

Melissa gave him a look. "With Doc's inventions? You're kidding, right?"

"Come on." Sean was already on his feet and heading for the door. "Let's go."

5

A Little Run-in

SATURDAY, 13:03 PDST

Slobs was in high gear. She galloped down Oak Street, doing what must have been thirty miles an hour . . . pulling Sean right behind her on his skateboard.

Melissa was struggling to keep up on her Rollerblades but losing ground every second. "Come on, guys!" she shouted. "Wait up!"

But if Sean heard, he didn't let on. His mind was on only one thing—getting to Doc's house as fast as possible to borrow Domesticus IV. He was so focused that he didn't notice how quickly they approached the busy intersection of Ninth Avenue. If he had, he might have slowed the big dog down a little.

Meanwhile, a long black limousine was racing north on Ninth, heading for the very same intersection.

Sean was closing in fast.

So was the limousine.

Suddenly Sean saw something he had never seen before. A stop sign! Wait a minute! When did that happen? Wasn't it the traffic on Ninth Avenue that had to stop?

But there it was, big and red, and getting closer and closer and . . .

"Slobs! Slow down, girl, slow!"

Slobs cocked her head to listen. Was her master yelling "Go!" or "Slow!"? But since Sean never did anything slow (except wake up), she figured he wanted her to *go*. So go she did—faster than ever!

Even from a half block back, Melissa could see her brother heading for trouble. "Stop sign!" she yelled. "Sean, there's a stop—"

Too late! He went shooting past the sign and into the street . . . right in front of the limo!

"Sean . . . look out!"

Sean let go of Slobs' leash. The dog swerved to the left, and the skateboard swerved to the right. Unfortunately, Sean's swerver must have been broken. He flew off the skateboard, shooting straight ahead like a human cannonball.

"EEYOWWW!"

SCREEECCCHHH!

Smoke poured out of the limousine's tires as they gripped the road and Sean crashed onto the street right in front of it.

"OOOAAFFFF!!"

He looked up to see the big car barreling down on him. He covered his eyes, clenched his teeth, and decided now was a good time to make sure everything was cool between him and God . . . since they'd no doubt be meeting face-to-face very, very soon.

Sean opened his eyes. It was dark. He didn't feel any pain. But how was that possible? Wait a minute! Maybe he really was dead!

Suddenly someone—or some*thing*—grabbed him by the ankle and began pulling.

The darkness disappeared, and Sean found himself looking up into the face of . . . something terrible! It had huge, bushy eyebrows growing over small, bloodshot eyes. Well, actually, they weren't eyebrows, more like eye*brow*. The creature had a single eyebrow that ran from one side of its forehead to the other. It wore superthick glasses, and a scar ran along the left jaw of its white, chalky-looking face. In contrast with the white face, the lips were almost too red, and the ears almost seemed pointed.

"Oh no," Sean moaned. "If I'm dead, I didn't make it to heaven!"

"Is he okay, Mortimer?" a woman's voice asked.

"Yes, ma'am," the creature answered. "He seems to be all right."

And then, leaning closer to Sean, it asked, "You are okay, aren't you, kid?"

Before Sean could answer, Slobs was suddenly on top of him, covering his face with slobbery kisses.

"Ewwww . . . Down, girl, down! That's enough!"

When he finally turned his face away, he saw his concerned sister. Standing next to her, looking just as concerned (in a monster sort of way), was the pale-faced creature apparently called Mortimer. That was when Sean noticed the much-too-small chauffeur's cap on top of Mortimer's head.

"Are you okay?" Melissa asked.

"I thought I was dead," Sean said. He sat up, then rose to his feet, dusting himself off. "I mean . . . it was all dark . . . and then someone grabbed me, and . . ."

"It was dark because you were under the car," Melissa explained. "That's how close you really came to getting run over. Mortimer here pulled you out."

Mortimer took off his hat and gave a polite half bow.

"Pleased to meet you," he said. "Glad we didn't kill you."

"Yeah," Sean nodded as he checked for various bruises and broken bones. "Me too." When he looked back up, he saw the limousine . . . and a beautiful raven-haired woman inside.

"Are you sure you are okay?" the woman asked. She had a thick eastern European accent.

Sean crossed over to her, still dusting himself off. "Yes, ma'am, I'm—" That's when he caught a glimpse inside her car. And that's when he went crazy. "Wow!" he cried. "Will you look at all that stuff!"

He had never seen so many electrical, state-of-the-art gadgets in his life. The entire back section of the limo was alive with flashing lights, beeping beepers, and more computers than at a Radio Shack sale. Whoever this woman was, she was something! It was impressive enough that she rode in a stretch limo with her own driver, but then to have all of that computer equipment . . .

"This is cool!" Sean exclaimed. "What do you do with all this?"

"Sean!" Melissa scolded. "Honestly, sometimes you can be so nosy."

The woman laughed the sweetest, gentlest laugh. It was almost musical. "I don't mind," she said. The accent made her sound even more elegant. "My name is Anna Montrose, and I have come a very, very long way. Could you please tell me where I might find your town hall? You see, I must—"

Before she finished, an electronic voice cut in. "Activity in Vector Twelve! Activity in Vector Twelve!"

It came from the computer screen inside the limo. Actually, it came from a face on that screen . . . a strange, leprechaun-like face that seemed to pulsate different colors as it spoke. First red, then green, now blue.

Sean was astonished. It looked exactly like Jeremiah . . . except for the long, curly red, er, now it was green, now it was blue, whatever-color-it-was, hair. Then there were those fluttery eyelashes and full red lips. In other words . . . it was a girl!

"Hey!" Jeremiah called from Sean's wristwatch. "Who's that? Hey! Hey!"

Sean glanced down at his watch and scowled. But Jeremiah would not be put off. "Lift me up so I can talk to her. Come on, come on, come on."

Fortunately, Anna was too busy worrying about that activity in Vector Twelve to notice Jeremiah.

"Come on," Jeremiah insisted. "Let me see, let me see!"

Hoping it would keep him quiet, Sean obeyed. Cautiously, he raised his wristwatch so Jeremiah could see the screen inside the car. It was love at first sight.

"Hi, there, sweetheart!" Jeremiah cooed.

The female image on the screen did not respond.

Jeremiah disappeared for an instant, then returned, clutching a bouquet of electronic carnations in his hand.

Still no response.

Jeremiah disappeared again and returned, wearing a tuxedo and holding a book of poetry.

Oh brother, Sean thought.

Jeremiah cleared his throat and began to read:

> "*Roses are red, violets are blue,*
> *On sale at Sears, a buck ninety-two.*"

No response.

He tried again:

> "*How do I love thee? Let me count the ways,*
> *No payments needed until ninety days.*"

Good grief! The poor guy was even worse at love poetry than he was at proverbs. Proverbs he generally got twisted around a little bit. But his love poetry . . . As best Sean could tell, he'd gotten it mixed up with an old Sears catalog!

"Mortimer!" Anna suddenly looked up from the computer screen and called, "We must go at once!"

"Coming, ma'am."

Mortimer started toward the limo, then suddenly stopped and screamed, "Yeeeeee!"

"What's wrong?" Sean cried.

"A frog!" the big man shrieked. "There's a frog!"

Sure enough, something big and green was lying on the street.

Sean bent down and picked it up. "It's only a leaf," he said.

"Oh, thank goodness," Mortimer sighed. "I'm sorry. It's just that frogs . . ."

"He's terrified of frogs," Anna explained. "He was frightened by one when he was a little boy."

"It jumped into my shorts and I couldn't get it out." Mortimer gave a shiver as he opened his door and got into the limo.

Sean and Melissa traded looks, trying not to laugh. It was pretty weird seeing a big, tough guy like Mortimer scared to death by something as harmless as a frog. Or, in this case, a leaf.

"Now, where did you kids say that town hall was?" Anna asked.

Sean pointed down the street. "Just go two more blocks."

"Thank you. Here." She thrust her business card at Melissa. It missed Melissa's hand and fluttered to the street. But the woman had no time to wait. "Drive, Mortimer," she cried. "Drive!"

The car lurched forward, and just like that, they were gone.

Sean could only stare after them as Melissa reached down to pick up the business card. When she turned it over, it read,

Anna Montrose—Vampire Fighter

Sean wanted to go straight to the town hall to see what was going on, but Melissa reminded him they still had chores to do. This didn't exactly make him leap for joy . . . until he remembered they were going to borrow Domesticus IV. Who knew, maybe doing chores wouldn't be so bad after all.

When they got to Doc's lab, she was already waiting for them. *How did you get here so fast?* She typed her question on a nearby keyboard, and it appeared on one of the several monitors.

"What do you mean?" Melissa asked.

I just sent you an e-mail a minute ago, Doc signed.

"E-mail?" Sean asked. "What e-mail?"

So you didn't get the message?

"No, we don't know what you're talking about."

Well, then. I have something very interesting to tell you. I've finished analyzing that piece of cloth you brought me.

"And?"

And there is only one place in the entire world that makes this type of material.

"Which is?" Sean asked.

A small factory . . . in Transylvania.

"Oh no," Melissa groaned.

"What?" Sean asked.

"Transylvania," Melissa swallowed. "That's where Count Dracula came from."

"So?" Sean asked.

"So . . ." She took a deep breath. "All the legends say Count Dracula was the first vampire."

6

Being a Detective Can Stink!

SATURDAY, 14:08 PDST

WHAT . . . WOULD . . . YOU . . . LIKE . . . ME . . . TO . . . DO . . . FIRST . . . SIR? Domesticus IV bowed low, clanking as he did.

"Let me think." Sean plopped down on the sofa. "I guess you can start by making my bed."

VERY . . . GOOD . . . SIR!

"Then the laundry, the dishes, and the vacuuming."

WILL . . . THAT . . . BE . . . ALL . . . SIR?

Sean shrugged. "Yeah, I guess. Oh . . . except maybe you can also mow the lawn."

"Sean . . ." Melissa protested.

"Oh yeah, and then you can ask my sister if there's anything she needs you to do for her."

THANK . . . YOU . . . SIR . . . I . . . WILL . . . GET . . . RIGHT . . . TO . . . IT.

"I don't want him to do anything for me!" Melissa said. "I think you're asking for trouble, getting him to do all the work you should be doing."

Sean shrugged again. "You worry too much. He's going to be fine."

The metal butler clanked up the stairs to go to work. Moments later they could hear him moving and banging around above them.

"Maybe we should just go make sure that he's—"

"He's fine," Sean insisted. "Don't worry about it."

After a few seconds, Domesticus came tromping back down the stairs with a basket full of laundry in his arms.

"See?" Sean said. "He's going to be great. Now, come on. We've got to do some thinking about this case." He motioned for his sister to sit. "Let's go back over all the clues."

"Okay," said Melissa. "First Mrs. Tubbs was attacked by a vampire."

"Somebody she *thought* was a vampire," Sean corrected.

"Whatever. And then I found that cloth . . ."

"Which Doc says is from Transylvania . . . the place where the vampire legend began."

They heard the vacuum cleaner roar to life in the den,

and Sean smiled. Yes, sir! This Domesticus IV was *some* great invention.

"Then," Melissa continued down the list of clues, "KC and the guys told us they'd seen movers carrying a coffin into the old Zanker place."

Sean nodded. "And when we went to check it out for ourselves, the vampire came out and—wait a minute!"

"What?" Melissa asked.

"Aren't vampires supposed to melt if they come out into the daylight?"

"Are they?" she asked. "Maybe you're thinking about the Wicked Witch of the West."

Sean shook his head. "No . . . I'm pretty sure that's vampires."

The vacuum cleaner switched off, and Domesticus clanked through the living room on his way to the kitchen.

"Is he done already?" Melissa asked.

"He works fast, doesn't he?" Sean smiled, then turned his attention back to the clues. "And then there's Anna and that creepy-looking driver of hers."

"She's got such an interesting accent," Melissa said. "I wonder where she's from?"

Sean shrugged. "Got me."

From the kitchen came the clanking of dishes—for about ten seconds. Then Domesticus came back through the living room, disappeared into the den, and once again, the vacuum cleaner clicked on.

"Does he seem to be moving faster to you?" Melissa asked.

"Faster? What do you mean . . . faster?"

The vacuum cleaner switched off and the robot appeared again. This time he practically ran into the kitchen.

"I mean faster," Melissa said. "Every time he comes through here, he seems to be moving faster than the last time."

"Yeah, well maybe . . ." Sean gave a nervous swallow. "Maybe he's just quick."

"And he's getting quicker all the time!"

Covered in soapsuds, Domesticus breezed out of the kitchen. His arms were full of dishes as he raced past them and into the laundry room.

"Sean?!"

"Okay, okay, I'll do something." Sean ran toward the kitchen to check. But before he got there, he was met by a mass of soap bubbles. He came to a stop and watched as they poured out of the kitchen and curled around his feet.

"Oh no," Melissa cried. She ran past him and sloshed her way into the kitchen. "Sean!" she yelled. "He put the laundry in the dishwasher!"

"Well, anybody can make a little mistake."

"And he used an entire box of detergent!"

"*Two* mistakes?"

CLINK! CLANK! BANG! CRASH!

Melissa slid out of the kitchen and listened. "What in the world. . . ?"

Suddenly they both shouted at the same time, "The dishes!"

They ran for the laundry room. But by the time they entered, it was too late. Domesticus had already loaded the washing machine with the dirty plates, cups, and glasses and had just turned it on:

CLINK! CLINK! CLINK!!
CLANK! CLANK! CLANK!!
CRASH! CRASH! CRASH!!

Sean lunged for the washer to turn it off. But by then most of the dishes were already broken.

WHIRRRRRR!

It was the vacuum cleaner again!

The two raced into the den and gasped. The vacuum cleaner's hose lay in the fish tank, and Dad's two prize goldfish, William and Mary, were nowhere to be seen.

Neither was Domesticus . . . although the back door was standing wide open.

Sean tore the bag out of the vacuum cleaner and ripped it open. An oozing pile of mud and lint fell onto the carpet. Fortunately, two little clumps of mud and lint were wiggling and jiggling about, fighting for breath.

With Melissa's help, Sean scooped them up and dumped them back into the aquarium. When he finally turned around, Domesticus was standing in the door. He held Dad's electric razor in one hand and something else in the other. What was it? A hamster? A rat?

IDIDWHATYOUSAID. He was talking much faster, sounding as if he were breathing helium!

"What I said?" Sean repeated.

"Meow," said the hamster or rat or whatever it was.

"Meow?" Melissa repeated nervously. "Was that a meow?"

IVACUUMEDTHEGOLDFISHANDSHAVEDTHE NEIGHBOR'SCAT.

"Oh no!" Melissa cried. "Tell me you didn't say, 'shaved the neighbor's cat'!"

OKAYIWON'T.

"Meow!"

But he had.

And without his thick, luxurious fur, Precious looked like he ought to be doing commercials for Taco Bell.

GOODBYE, said Domesticus IV.

"No, wait. . . !" Sean shouted.

IMUSTMOWTHENEIGHBORHOOD.

"No!"

THENIWILLBEBACKTOFIXYOUSOMESOAPAND SANDWICHESFORLUNCH.

He turned and ran out the door.

Sean spun around to his sister and cried, "Did he say 'soap and sandwiches'?"

"Right after he mows the neighborhood!" Melissa shouted. "Come on, we've got to stop him!"

"Tell me something I don't know!" Sean shouted. "But how?"

VAROOOOM!

The lawn mower roared to life, and Domesticus IV came running out of the garage with it.

Sean and Melissa raced toward him, holding out their hands. But they might as well have tried to stop a freight train.

ZOOM!

He ran right around them, cutting a diagonal path across the lawn.

"Look out for. . . !"

ZIPPP . . .

But it was too late. Dad's morning glories were history.

ZIPPP . . .

So were Mrs. Tubbs' prized petunias!

Now he was heading straight for the Johnsons' fence. Maybe that would stop him!

CRASH!

Maybe not.

Unfortunately, Mr. Johnson had just resurfaced the driveway, and it wasn't quite dry yet.

GLOP! GLOP! GLOP!

Domesticus breezed through it as if it were soggy oatmeal! Next up was the . . .

K-RASH!

. . . prickly hedge on the other side of the yard.

"Ow! Ow! Ow!" Sean and Melissa followed right behind.

WHACK!

The Murrays' birdbath bit the dust.

SNAP!

So did their plastic pink flamingo.

And then, for no apparent reason, Domesticus IV turned around and headed back the way he came!

By this time Mrs. Tubbs had run outside to see what all the noise was about. She'd just stepped off her porch when the huge metallic monster came crashing back through the fence and into her yard.

"AGHHH!" She turned tail and started running, with good ol' Domesticus right behind.

Now, Mrs. Tubbs was kind of old, and she was pretty heavy. But you wouldn't have known it by the way she ran! They raced across the Garcias' freshly fertilized lawn. (YUCK!)

Through the Browns' cactus garden. (OUCH!)

And . . .

"Mrs. Tubbs! Look out!"

Too late!

KER-SPLASH!

She landed face first in the Rutherfords' fishpond.

But not Domesticus IV. He stopped dead still at the edge of the pond as Mrs. Tubbs crawled out of the water, coughing and sputtering.

WOULD . . . YOU . . . LIKE . . . ME . . . TO . . . DRY . . . THOSE . . . CLOTHES? Domesticus reached a steel claw out toward the woman. That was all it took. The poor lady leaped to her feet and set a world speed record running down the street.

Huffing and puffing, Sean and Melissa finally arrived at the pond.

"You stopped!" Sean cried.

I . . . AM . . . SORRY . . . SIR . . . BUT . . . IT . . . SEEMS . . . THE . . . LAWN . . . MOWER . . . HAS . . . RUN . . . OUT . . . OF . . . GAS.

"Yes!" Melissa shouted.

I . . . SEEM . . . TO . . . BE . . . LOW . . . ON . . . GAS . . . MYSELF. WILL . . . THAT . . . BE . . . ALL . . . SIR? HAVE . . . I . . . DONE . . . ENOUGH?

"Done enough?" Sean yelled. "Done enough?" He looked back at the trail of wreckage Domesticus had left behind. "It will take me years to pay for all this!"

VERY . . . GOOD . . . SIR. I. . . . SEEM. . . . .TO. . . . BE. . . . . . . IN. . . . . . . NEED. . . . . OF. . . . . A. . . . . NAAAAAAP . . .

The last word was long and drawn out as the lights on his digital display grew dimmer and dimmer, until they finally blinked out completely.

Sean shuffled along with his shoulders slouched and his hands stuffed in his pockets. He and Melissa were on their way to the town hall to see what Anna Montrose was up to. Slobs walked silently between them.

"Come on," Melissa urged him. "Domesticus didn't do that much damage."

Sean gave her a look. "Oh yes, he did."

Still trying to cheer him up, she changed the subject. "Hey! Maybe you'll get to see all those cool gadgets in that limo again."

Sean shrugged. "I guess that wouldn't be so bad."

"Not so bad! Not so bad!!" It was Jeremiah speaking from Sean's wristwatch again. "It'll be great! I'll get to see *her* again!"

"Oh, there you are," Melissa said. "You've really fallen for that little person, haven't you?"

"Ahh," he sighed. "It was love at first bite."

Melissa tried not to giggle. "You mean love at first sight."

But before Jeremiah could answer, Slobs suddenly stopped, put her nose to the air, and began sniffing furiously.

"What is it, girl?" Sean asked.

"Ew!" Melissa cried. "I smell it, too! It's horrible!"

Now Sean did. "Ugh! What is that?"

Just then KC, Spalding, and Bear came walking around the corner, each wearing a necklace of giant garlic cloves.

"You guys stink," Sean said, covering his mouth and nose. "What are you doing?"

"What does it look like we're doing?" KC snapped back. "We're keeping the vampires away."

"What?" Melissa asked.

"It is common knowledge that vampires do not remain in the presence of garlic," Spalding explained.

Melissa stepped back and held her nose. "I don't blame them!"

"You guys would be wearing garlic, too," Bear said, "if you knew what was good for you."

"Where are you going?" KC asked.

"Down to the town hall," Sean said.

"Us too," KC said. "We heard there's some kind of meeting going on there. Let's go check it out."

There must have been four hundred people gathered in front of the town hall, and nearly *all* of them wore garlic. In fact, it smelled like every Italian restaurant in the world had set up shop there!

"I guess I was wrong when I said nobody listens to Ricardo Ruelas," Sean said.

"Yeah," Melissa agreed as they passed someone carrying a sign reading *Save Our City From*

Bloodsuckers. "It looks like everybody's pretty worked up."

Eventually the kids managed to work their way through the crowd and into the building. As they passed the mayor's office, they could hear the receptionist on the phone trying to calm someone down:

"I promise we'll send somebody to check on it! Yes, I understand. First a vampire . . . and now a big metallic creature from Mars. All the monsters want to destroy you. Of course I believe you, Mrs. Tubbs. . . ."

Melissa shook her head. Poor Mrs. Tubbs.

The kids made their way down the hall to the town council meeting room, where Anna Montrose was speaking. Several TV monitors were spaced throughout the room for those who couldn't squeeze in close enough to get a good view.

Some of her fancy gadgetry was spread out on the table before her, with lights flashing and blinking. Mortimer, the chauffeur, stood off to one side.

"I tell you," Anna was saying, "this town is under attack! I have chased the vampires all the way from the old country, and they are intent on destroying Midvale. They want to turn you all into bloodsucking monsters!"

Anna was a powerful speaker, and the audience seemed to hang on every word. There was also something about those blinking lights. They were so . . . captivating. Almost . . . hypnotic.

She went on. "I know how to build a machine that will get rid of the vampires." She gestured at the equipment sitting on the table in front of her. "As you can see, I am very close to completing my work. All it needs is your basic double-flux magneto capacitor and a cathode ray debilitator. But as I am sure you know, both of those items are very expensive."

The people exchanged understanding nods as if they really knew what she was talking about.

"What's a 'cathode ray debilitator'?" Melissa whispered.

Sean rolled his eyes. "You wouldn't understand," he whispered back. "You're just a girl."

Melissa put her hands on her hips. "What's *that* got to do with anything? Girls aren't stupid, you know. And *I've* never heard of a 'cathode ray debilitator' or a 'magneto cap-whatzit.' "

"Shh!" Sean motioned for her to be quiet.

Back onstage, Anna began to dab her eyes. "I've spent every penny I had on this machine," she sobbed. "But I'm still ten thousand dollars short. That's all I need to finish my work and rid this town—nay, the entire world—of vampires once and for all!"

"I'll give fifty dollars!" someone shouted.

"Me too!"

"Here's a hundred right now!"

Soon, people from all over the room were crowding forward and shoving their money at Anna, who gladly accepted it.

That was when the love of Jeremiah's life suddenly appeared on the monitors. "Activity in Vector Twelve," she said.

Jeremiah spotted her from Sean's watch and couldn't contain himself. Once again he had to recite some poetry:

"My love, it is like a red, red rose!
So whack me with a lifetime-guaranteed garden hose!"

A hush fell over the room.

"What was that?" someone cried.

"It didn't sound human!" another shouted.

"It's me!" Jeremiah yelled. "I'm in love! And I want the whole world to know!"

Suddenly he was everywhere! On every monitor. Anna's face had been replaced on the screens by Jeremiah's dazzling image. And it *was* dazzling. Melissa had never seen him change colors so fast!

"Look!" someone cried. "It's . . ."

"A vampire!" another yelled.

"A monster!" someone shouted.

"Let me out of here!"

"Me too!"

Suddenly everyone was stampeding toward the exits, yelling and screaming for their very lives.

Melissa breathed an impatient sigh and looked at her watch for the hundredth time in five minutes. She and Sean had been standing in the parking lot outside the town hall for over an hour, waiting for a chance to talk to Anna and Mortimer.

"Sean," Melissa whined, "maybe we should just—"

"Here they come!" he interrupted. "Miss Montrose . . . Mortimer. Can we talk to you for a minute?"

"I'm sorry, children," Anna said, "we're in a very big hurry and—" Suddenly she stopped. "Oh, you're the boy we almost ran over. Are you all right?"

"Fine, ma'am."

"Good. Well, as I said, we're in a hurry, so—"

"We just wanted to tell you that we have a detective agency," Sean said.

"Bloodhounds, Inc.," Melissa added.

"And we've been hired to find this vampire that's been scaring everybody. So we figured maybe we could give you a hand and—"

"Hold it a minute, kiddies," Mortimer said. "Ms. Montrose doesn't need any help."

"I understand, but—"

"Mortimer's right," Anna said, her pleasant voice suddenly just a little less pleasant. "The last thing I need is you two getting in my way."

"But we just thought—"

"You want to help me," she snapped. "Then stay out of my hair."

With that, the two brushed past Sean and Melissa. But they'd taken only a step or two before Anna turned back, suddenly all smiles and sweetness again. "Don't worry about the vampires, children. We're professionals; we'll get rid of them."

She turned and continued walking away.

Sean and Melissa traded looks. Something was fishy about these two. Very, very fishy.

7

Who's Biting My Neck?

FRIDAY, 15:27 PDST

"Hey, wait up!"

Sean and Melissa were heading home from school when they turned to see KC, Spalding, and Bear hurrying after them.

The last couple weeks had been pretty strange, even by Midvale standards. There was at least one vampire attack every night, and sometimes two. Anna had set up a box at the town hall, where citizens of Midvale could contribute money to help her build her vampire-killing machine. And each attack brought in even bigger contributions.

Luckily, no one had ever been hurt by the vampire, although sometimes he stole money, jewels, or other valuables.

Then there was that huge bat—with glowing eyes and whirring wings—that almost always showed up outside the victims' houses just before the vampire made his entrance. Although Sean and Melissa had been working hard on the case, they still weren't anywhere close to solving it.

"You guys doing anything after school?" KC asked as they arrived.

"Just the usual fifty hours of homework," Melissa sighed. "Why?"

"We're gonna go back over to the Zanker place," KC croaked in her raspy little voice. "Thought maybe you'd like to go with us."

"We already did that," Sean said.

"Perhaps," Spalding sniffed and pushed up his glasses. "However, this time it shall be entirely different."

"Different?" Melissa asked. "How?"

KC answered, "We're gonna go right up on the porch; then we're gonna knock on the door. And when that old creep answers it, we're gonna ask him right to his face if he's the vampire!"

Sean laughed. "Great idea! And of course, he'll admit it."

"There is no end to the speculation of what his response may be," Spalding replied. "But this time we will be quite prepared. Show them, Bear."

"You bet." Bear opened his jacket wide.

"What's that?" Melissa asked. "Why are you carrying around a two-by-four in your coat?"

"It's not a two-by-four!" KC croaked. "It's a wooden stake!"

"A stake?"

"Certainly." Spalding lowered his voice. "To drive through the vampire's heart."

Sean shook his head. "You guys have been watching way too many *Buffy* episodes."

"You know a better way to get rid of a vampire?"

"I don't believe in vampires," Sean said.

"Oh yeah . . ." KC challenged him. "You weren't so sure a few days ago. What changed your mind?"

Sean shrugged. "I know I got a little spooked. But I believe what the Bible says—dead people either go to heaven or . . . you know . . . the other place. If that's true, then there's no such thing as a vampire. There's got to be a natural explanation for all of this."

"Then you won't be needing these?" Bear reached into his coat pocket and pulled out two brand-new garlic necklaces. "I made 'em just for you guys."

Sean shook his head. "Thanks, but we'll pass."

"Actually," Melissa said, reaching out for one, "maybe it wouldn't hurt—just to be safe."

"Misty!" Sean looked at her, surprised.

"Well . . . everybody else is wearing them."

"You don't need it, remember? 'The one who is in you is greater . . .' "

"Oh yeah." Melissa gave a nervous chuckle as she handed the necklace back to Bear.

"Your funeral," Bear said.

KC continued. "So if you ain't afraid of vampires, then you ain't afraid of going back to Zanker's with us, right?"

Sean shrugged. "Sure, why not?"

"Then let's proceed with great haste," Spalding suggested.

With that, the group turned and everyone started toward the old house. Well, everyone but Melissa.

"Hey, Misty," KC called. "Ain't you comin'?"

"No, I, uh . . . homework. Yeah, that's it, I've got way too much homework. You guys go ahead. I've got to get home and start studying."

Sean gave her a look. It was Friday. He knew it had nothing to do with homework. Instead, her refusal to go had everything to do with fear.

"Well, suit yourself," KC called.

They headed for the house, leaving Melissa feeling a little foolish and a lot alone.

Here they were again . . . standing across the street from the old Zanker place, trying to work up their nerve.

"So what are we waitin' for?" Bear complained.

"Actually, you are the one possessing the stake," Spalding answered. "Perhaps you should proceed to the door and announce your presence first."

Bear looked up at the old house, which, as the clouds began to cover the sun, was getting spookier by the moment. "I dunno," he said. "It didn't seem so scary when we thought about it at school."

"What about you?" KC pointed at Sean. "If you've got so much courage . . . you go on up and knock on the door."

Sean swallowed, took a deep breath, and finally nodded. "All right, I will." With every ounce of faith and courage he could muster, he started toward the old house.

"He's goin'!" KC whispered excitedly. "Come on!"

The other three followed. As long as Sean was willing to lead, they were willing to follow—just not too closely.

Sean started up the rickety porch steps.

CREEAAAK!

That was all it took to send the other three scurrying back out into the street.

Sean turned to them and scorned, "That was just an old step."

"Okay . . . okay," KC whispered. "We're coming."

Sean continued up the steps . . .

CREAK . . .
CRACK . . .
CROAK . . .
GROAN . . .

. . . each one sounding worse than the last.

Finally he arrived on the porch. Then, with shaking hand, he reached up to knock on the door. But as his knuckles hit the wood, the strangest thing happened:

EEEEEEERRRRR. . . .

"Look!" KC cried. "The door's opening."

"You know," Sean gulped, "maybe Misty needs a hand with all of that homework."

"What, are you chicken?" KC taunted.

"Of course not."

"Well?" She gestured toward the open door. "What are you waiting for?"

Sean had no choice. He had to continue or be branded a chicken the rest of his life. Ever so slowly, he opened the door just a little wider and stuck his head inside. "Hello?" he called. "Anybody home?"

There was no answer.

"Let's go inside," KC croaked.

"What, are you crazy?" Sean asked.

"Maybe they're hurt," Bear said. "Or maybe they need our help, or maybe, or maybe—"

"—or maybe you're just nuts," Sean concluded.

"Well, if you ain't going, I am," KC said. Suddenly she sounded very brave. (The fact that all the others were right beside her probably didn't hurt.) A moment later all four stood in the entry hall. The house was silent, except for the loud ticking of a nearby clock.

"Hello. . . ?" KC called.

Still no answer. Up ahead, an open door revealed steps leading down to the basement. It was hard to tell which was worse—their fear or their curiosity. But they had gone this far. Carefully, they inched their way to the stairs and looked down them into the darkness.

"I don't see nothin'," Bear whispered.

"Shh . . ." Spalding said.

"Maybe we should go down and look," Bear suggested.

"Right," KC scoffed. "And maybe we should just call up the cemetery and tell them to start digging our graves right now. I tell you, Bear, sometimes—"

"There it is!" Spalding pointed.

"Where?" Sean asked.

"Right there, in the corner!"

All eyes followed his finger. He was right. There was something there in the shadows. Something that looked exactly like . . . a coffin.

For the longest moment, no one said a word. To be honest, Sean wasn't sure he could speak if he wanted to.

Suddenly KC whispered, "What's that?"

Sean strained to listen.

K-thump . . . K-thump . . . K-thump

It sounded like footsteps. And they were getting louder. Someone—or some*thing*—was sneaking up behind them. They spun around toward the front door, thinking of making a run for it, when suddenly . . .

K-BAMB!

. . . the door slammed shut!

Back home, Melissa was lying on her bed, rubbing her tired eyes and feeling like a major coward for not going with Sean. True, she really did have homework, including having to read some scary short story by an author named Edgar Allan Poe. But still . . .

With a heavy sigh she picked the book back up. Let's

see, how many pages had she read so far? Only twelve? She had thirty more to go! She groaned and went back to reading when suddenly she noticed how cold the room was. Maybe she ought to get up and close the window.

Wait a minute. The window *was* closed!

Then why were her curtains blowing like that? And what was that thing coming in through her window?

Thing coming in through her window?!?

It was a bat! A vampire bat! It landed on her windowsill and sat there eyeing her with its small red eyes until . . .

POOF!

The not-so-cute bat was now an even not-so-cuter man . . . who'd suddenly . . .

K-BONK!

. . . hit his head on the top of the window when he'd transformed himself.

"Man, that hurts!" he grumbled. "I gotta remember to wait until I'm inside before I do that."

Melissa watched from her bed, trembling like Jell-O on a jackhammer during an earthquake when . . .

WHAM!

. . . the window fell down on the cape. The man turned

around and tugged at it, trying to get free. "I ruin more good capes that way," he whined.

Finally he got free, turned, and started toward Melissa.

She tried to move but was paralyzed with fear. She reached for the garlic necklace around her neck . . . until she remembered Sean had made her give it back to Bear.

The vampire came closer.

She swallowed.

And closer.

She tried to scream, but no sound would come.

And closer some more.

Her heart pounded in her chest. She could barely breathe as she watched him bend over her. Now she could feel his hot breath on her neck. She closed her eyes and silently began to pray.

8

My Vampire Has Fleas

The vampire's breath was horrible. He smelled like . . . like . . . Alpo.

Now his fangs were upon her neck. Paralyzed with fear, she braced herself and waited for the pain of his bite. But instead of sharp and painful, it was cold and wet. In fact, it was downright slobbery!

He began licking her all over her face—long, drooling licks.

"Bad vampire," Melissa moaned. "Down, vampire, down!" Until her eyes blinked open and she saw . . .

"Slobs!" she cried. "What are you doing here?"

Melissa pushed the big dog away, sat up in bed, and looked around the room. There was no sign of any vampire. Her window was shut tight. On the bed beside her, opened to page 23, was Edgar Allan Poe's "Premature Burial."

"I must have been asleep!" she giggled nervously. "Oh, Slobs, thank you! Thank you for waking me up."

She wrapped her arms around the big bloodhound, who wagged her tail happily and managed to get in one more juicy, drooly . . .

SLURP!

Unfortunately, Sean was not dreaming. He had been standing on top of the basement stairs looking down when the front door had slammed shut. And now someone—or some*thing*—was closing in on them.

Closer and closer the footsteps came.

K-thump . . . K-thump . . . K-thump

Sean raced to the door, trying to open it. But it was locked. He fumbled with it, pulling at it for all he was worth, but it did no good.

"What are we going to do?" cried Spalding.

"I don't know!" shouted KC.

"Hide!" yelled Bear.

It sounded like a pretty good idea. And since there

was really no place to go but down the stairs, that's where they ran. Although it wasn't really running. It was more like . . .

BAMB BAMB BAMB
BOUNCE BOUNCE BOUNCE
"OUCH!" "OUCH!" "OUCH!"

. . . falling . . . down the stairs . . . one person on top of another.

Spalding was the first to leap back up to his feet. Which was good, except for the part where he tripped and fell face first over the pile of kids.

"OAFF!"

Bear was next. Same leaping up, same falling down. But since he was a lot heavier, it meant a lot harder fall.

"OAFF!"

KC and Sean were the final contestants. They'd gotten up and made it as far as the stairs before they managed to fall over each other. That's when a figure emerged from the top of the stairs. It was hard for them to get a good look at him, but they didn't have to. They all knew who he was:

The vampire! It was too late! Now there was no hope of escape!

And then he spoke. "What are you kids doing in my basement?"

"Noth-noth-nothing, sir," KC stuttered.

"We mean no harm!" Spalding cried.

"Please don't bite us!" Bear screamed.

"Bite you?" the vampire asked. "Why would I want to bite you?"

"So you can suck out all our blood," KC explained.

The "creature" started down the stairs. But as each step brought him closer, the kids stepped farther back . . . until they were up against the far wall.

"Suck your blood?" the creature asked. "What in the world are you talking about?"

"That's what vampires do," Spalding said.

"Vampires? Are you out of your minds? Who said anything about vampires?"

The creature arrived at the bottom of the stairs and turned on the basement light. Now, at last, everyone could see him clearly. . . .

He was a short, white-haired gentleman with a neatly trimmed beard. He wore a flannel shirt, khaki pants, and glasses that came down so far on his nose that he had to look over them. On his head was a Boston Red Sox cap, and around his waist was tied an apron.

Vampire? Sean thought. *This guy looks more like Santa Claus than a vampire.*

"To be frank," Spalding admitted, "you certainly don't look like a vampire."

"Well, thank you for that," the old man chuckled. He took off his baseball cap and scratched his head. "What on earth gave you the crazy idea that I was?"

"We saw your coffin," Sean explained.

"My *what*?"

"We looked through the window and we saw your coffin." Sean pointed. "That one, over there."

The old man chuckled again . . . until it turned into a laugh . . . until he threw back his head and really let loose.

The kids glanced nervously at one another.

When he finally stopped, the old man dabbed at his eyes and started toward the coffin. "Here," he said, "let me show you something."

The kids followed, cautiously.

When he arrived, he stooped down and grabbed one end of it. "Here," he said, "give me a hand with this."

Sean bent down and helped him lift it until it was sitting up on its end. Suddenly it no longer looked like a coffin. Now it looked a lot more like a . . . a grandfather clock!

"Isn't it beautiful?" the old man said. "Made especially for the king of Prussia in 1832."

"Wow," Sean said. "So you . . ."

". . . collect antique furniture. Especially clocks," the man said. "That's why I bought this old house. It seemed like the perfect place to open an antique shop."

KC snapped her fingers. "So that explains all the creepy . . . er . . . I mean, all the old furniture."

The man nodded. "I even had some flyers printed up. The day I saw you kids, I was going to ask you to pass them out . . . but you took off running."

Sean nodded. "We're sorry, Mr. . . ."

"O'Riley. Caleb O'Riley."

He stuck out his hand, and Sean took it. "I'm pleased to meet you, Mr. O'Riley. Very, *very* pleased."

FRIDAY 19:21 PDST

"So now we know the old guy's not the vampire," Melissa said. "That's good. But where does it leave us?"

Sean sighed. "I was kind of hoping you'd have an idea."

"Sorry. All out."

They sat silently in Melissa's bedroom for several moments. They would have sat in Sean's bedroom, but it was impossible to find a chair, or the bed, or the floor for that matter. Sean's a little bit of a slob. Actually, he's a big bit of a slob.

He sighed again. "Maybe we ought to go back over the clues. We're missing something, I'm sure of it."

They turned to stare at the map of Midvale that was

pinned to the corkboard. The location of every vampire attack was marked with a yellow *X*. Beneath each *X*, he and Melissa had written the date and time of the attack.

"Where is the vampire going to attack next?" Sean asked, speaking to nobody in particular.

Melissa nodded, rose to her feet, and began to pace. "If we could figure that out . . ."

". . . then we could be waiting for him," Sean concluded.

Several more moments passed before Melissa looked back to the map from across the room. That's when she gasped.

"What is it?" Sean asked. "What do you see?"

"Come here." She motioned to him. "We've been standing too close to the map to see it."

"To see what?" Sean asked as he rose to join her.

"Come look for yourself!"

When he did, his mouth fell open. Because from where they stood they could clearly see the unmistakable pattern of the vampire's attacks.

"It's a pentagram!" Sean exclaimed.

Melissa nodded. "A five-pointed star. But it's not quite finished!"

"It's still got one more point to go!" Sean exclaimed. "Quick, get the tape measure."

Melissa obeyed, and a moment later the two

detectives measured once . . . measured twice . . . and measured a third time, just to be sure. But each and every time, they came to the same conclusion. In order to complete the pentagram, the next attack would have to take place at 1411 Hudson Street.

"That's Bear's house!" Sean cried.

Melissa nodded. "But when?"

Sean looked back to the map and to the dates they'd written on it.

"Oh boy," he sighed.

"Oh boy, what?" Melissa demanded.

"The next attack is going to be tonight . . . and if it's the same time as the other attacks . . ." He looked at his watch. "Uh-oh."

"What?" Melissa asked.

"We've got forty-five minutes!"

"Forty-five minutes?!"

"Come on!" He started for the door. "We've got to hurry!"

FRIDAY, 20:14 PDST

"Sean," Melissa whispered, "it's almost time."

"I know."

The two of them sat in the darkness of Bear's bedroom, waiting for the vampire to appear. Slobs slept on the floor beside them, twitching in her sleep, no doubt dreaming her favorite dream—chasing Mrs. Tubbs' cat.

Bear's folks had gone out to a movie, and Bear the Unbrave suddenly remembered he was supposed to have a sleep-over at Spalding's. So there they were—Sean, Melissa, and Slobs—having to face the vampire all by themselves.

"Maybe it won't show," Melissa said hopefully.

Sean shook his head. "We want it to show, remember? That's why we're here."

"Oh yeah." Melissa tried to hide the fear in her voice. "Well, maybe it will come after we—"

But that's all she got out. Suddenly the window in Bear's room began to open and the curtains began to blow.

"All right," Sean whispered. "Right on schedule."

Something appeared floating just outside the window. Something that looked exactly like . . .

"It's the bat," Melissa said with a shiver. "The vampire bat!"

Sean nodded. There was no mistaking the glowing eyes and whirring wings.

Now it was time for the all-important question. The one Melissa had been meaning to ask all night. "Sean?"

"Yeah?"

"What do we do now?"

"Now?"

"Yes . . . *now!*"

"I, uh . . . I haven't figured that part out yet."

9

Truth Revealed

Any minute now, the big, ugly bat was going to transform itself into an even bigger and uglier vampire. Any minute now, he'd be coming through that window.

"Sean," Melissa cried, grabbing her brother's arm. "Do something!"

"Like what?"

"Like . . . anything. Surprise me!"

K-POW!

Suddenly an explosion filled Bear's bedroom with more smoke than when Dad tries to barbecue. With nothing else better to do than save their lives, the two hit the floor and hid behind the bed. When they came back up, the bat was gone.

Instead, standing in the middle of the room was . . . Anna Montrose!

And she was angry.

"I almost had him tonight!" she shouted. "But you kids got in the way!"

Sean and Melissa looked at her, not knowing what to say. Then they looked at each other, still not knowing what to say.

"Fighting vampires is serious business!" Anna yelled. "You must leave it to the experts! Do you understand me? You're going to get hurt if you don't stay out of the way!"

"But, Ms. Montrose," Melissa began, "we were only trying to—"

"If you want to help me, stay out of my way!"

FRIDAY, 20:37 PDST

The two detectives remained silent as they walked home through the dark streets of Midvale. They both thought about what they'd seen and what Anna Montrose had said.

Finally Melissa spoke. "She really was mad, wasn't she?"

"Yeah . . ."

More silence.

"So . . . are we going to do it?"

"Do what?" Sean asked.

"Stay out of it from now on?"

"I don't know. What do you think?"

"Well . . . I think we were solving crimes around here before she ever showed up. And if anybody ought to stay out of this, it's her."

Sean looked at her and smiled. "You know, for a little sister, you're not half bad . . . some of the time."

"Thanks."

"You're right," Sean continued. "You and me, we're the ones who started this case. And we're the ones who are going to solve it."

"And me, too," Jeremiah chimed in from Sean's watch. "Don't forget me."

"And you, too, Jeremiah," Sean chuckled.

"Woof!"

"Yes, and you, too, Slobs."

"But, Jeremiah," Melissa asked, "I thought you didn't want anything to do with this case. What made you change your mind?"

"*She* did," Jeremiah sighed. It was obvious thoughts of his electronic sweetheart were again filling his little microchips. "If I help you catch the vampire, then maybe I'll be her hero. We'll be just like Rumplestiltsken and Juliet."

"That's *Romeo* and Juliet," Melissa corrected him.

"Yeah, them, too," Jeremiah said. "By the way, you did know that vampire tonight wasn't real, didn't you?"

"Then what was it?" Melissa asked. "I mean, we saw it with our own eyes."

"It was there, but it wasn't real. At least it wasn't a real bat. Someone was operating it by remote control. Not only that, but it was taking video pictures and beaming back the information."

"How do you know all that?" Sean demanded.

"Elementary, my dear Walkman."

"That's *Watson*," Melissa corrected him.

"Whatever. Anyway, it was coming through on my frequency. Don't forget. I'm something of a broadcast transmission myself . . . and it takes one to tangle."

Melissa rolled her eyes. "The phrase is 'It takes two to tango.' But I think you mean 'It takes one to know one.' "

"Sending information where?" Sean asked. "And to who?"

"I've been trying to pinpoint the exact location," Jeremiah said, "but it keeps moving." Suddenly he disappeared from Sean's wristwatch, and a map of Midvale appeared. It grew closer and closer, until only a few blocks could be seen. And, moving down one of the streets, a small white dot was blinking on and off.

"They must have the transmitter in some sort of vehicle," Sean said.

Finally the white dot stopped moving. It blinked a few more times, then disappeared from the screen.

"We lost it," Melissa sighed.

"Maybe not," Jeremiah said. "Hang on, I'll be back in a flask." He disappeared, then reappeared, wearing a college cap and gown. He held a long, wooden pointer and was motioning to a chalkboard filled with a complex math formula.

"Let me see. If we take the speed at which the transmitter was traveling times the coefficient of *X* divided by pi—"

"Jeremiah," Sean interrupted.

". . . raise this to the fourteenth power . . ."

"Jeremiah?"

". . . find the square root of the hypotenuse of this right triangle . . ."

"Jeremiah!"

"Yes?"

"What are you doing?"

Suddenly information was typed across the bottom of the screen:

Broadcast transmission point of origin:
814 Myrtle Avenue

"Jeremiah," Melissa exclaimed, "you're a genius! Where did you learn that?"

"Oh, I was dating an electronic calculator there for a while and—"

"Myrtle Avenue?" Sean interrupted. "That's only a few blocks from here."

"That must be their hideout!" Melissa exclaimed.

"So what are we waiting for?" Sean asked. "Let's go!"

FRIDAY, 21:02 PDST

Myrtle Avenue was an ordinary street. And 814 was probably the most ordinary house on the ordinary block. A small white picket fence ran around it, and a swing set was in the backyard.

"You sure you got that address right?" Melissa whispered. "This doesn't look like the sort of place—"

"Never judge a book by the company it keeps," Jeremiah reminded her. He didn't quite have it right, but she knew what he meant: You can't judge by appearances. That was the lesson they'd already learned about the old Zanker place. Now it looked like they were about to put that lesson to use.

"You stay here," Sean whispered. "I'm going around back to see if I can check out what's going on in there."

"No way!" Melissa whispered. "I'm going with you!"

Sean turned to her. She had that look in her eyes—the one that said no matter what he tried to do, she wasn't leaving his side. Of course, he wasn't crazy about the idea. But he was even less crazy about getting into an argument right there in front of the house. "All right," he sighed. "Come on."

They approached the fence and he pushed open the gate.

Squeak

Sean froze, obviously waiting for the vampires or whoever to come out with their guns blazing. But there was nothing. No vampires. No blazing guns.

Good.

He continued forward. Melissa and Slobs stayed right on his heels. As they made their way around the side of the house, he could hear voices from inside—a man and a woman. They were laughing.

Suddenly Melissa let out a scream. "Eeee—"

Sean spun around just as she covered her mouth with her hand. "Sorry," she whispered. "I almost stepped on a frog."

He nodded. Girls—go figure.

They continued around the side of the house until they spotted a lit window in the back. Cautiously, they approached it.

Sean was the first to rise up and look inside.

There, sitting at the kitchen table, drinking champagne and carrying on with a huge pile of money in front of her was . . . Anna. And sitting across from her, dressed in a vampire suit, was . . . Mortimer!

A moment later Melissa had risen up to join Sean. She could only stare into the window with wide eyes. "I can't believe it," she whispered.

"Neither can I," Sean answered.

"Believe what?" Jeremiah squawked from Sean's watch. "I want to see."

"In a second," Sean whispered. "Let's hear what they're saying."

The three of them grew very quiet and held their breaths so they could hear the conversation.

"You were certainly right, my dear," Mortimer burped. "This town was the easiest one yet."

"I knew it would be," Anna nodded. "Except for those snoopy brats. But after tomorrow we won't have to worry about them anymore."

Mortimer raised his glass. "Then its back to Transylvania, where we can live like royalty!"

"Transylvania!" Melissa whispered. "So that's where her accent's from!"

"Shh," Sean said. "Keep listening."

"One more attack," Anna was saying. "And we will

retire from the vampire business for good."

Mortimer pushed away from the table, walked around behind Anna, and gently kissed her on top of the head. "And then finally we'll have enough money to retire."

"Ten long years," Anna sighed. "Ten years of playing this stupid vampire game. I'll be so glad when it's over."

"Me too," said Mortimer. "I'm not as young as I used to be. My acrobat days were a long time ago. Climbing up walls to get in upstairs windows is taking its toll."

"After tomorrow you'll never have to climb another wall, my dear," Anna said. "That, I can promise."

"But I have to admit, I'll kind of miss your magic tricks!"

Anna laughed. "Oh, no one says the magic has to end." With that, she produced a wad of flash paper, swept it past the flame of a lit candle, and . . .

POOF!

. . . a blinding flash filled the room. A flash exactly like they had seen in Bear's room.

"I want to see," Jeremiah whined. "Let me see what's happening."

"Okay," Sean finally agreed. "But I don't think you're going to like it."

Sean slowly lifted his wrist to the window and turned

it so Jeremiah could get a good view.

"I have to tell you," Mortimer laughed, "I just love your little Vector Twelve girl, too."

"Thank you," Anna said. "Isn't it amazing what you can do with computer clip art these days?" And then she began to call out, "Activity in Vector Twelve! Activity in Vector Twelve!"

Mortimer threw back his head and laughed. "I just love it when you do that voice," he said. "Sometimes I almost think she's real."

The information was more than Jeremiah's little printed circuits could handle. "She's a fake!" Jeremiah cried. "She's not even real!"

"What was that?" Mortimer said.

"Outside!" Anna shouted. "Someone's ouside!"

Sean glanced at his watch. Jeremiah was so upset that he was bouncing back and forth against the edges, growing brighter and brighter . . .

"Uh-oh," Sean whispered. "He's going to blow."

By now Mortimer had pulled a gun from his pocket and was rushing for the door.

But before he could get outside, a beam of electrical energy shot from Sean's watch and headed for the nearby circuit breaker on the outside wall of the house.

"Look out!" Sean cried as he and Melissa ducked for cover.

ZIIPPP . . .
K-RACKLE, K-RACKLE, K-RACKLE

Suddenly there were more sparks than the Fourth of July, followed by a loud . . .

K-BOOM!

. . . as the circuit breaker blew, and all house and yard lights went dark.

"Who's there?" Mortimer yelled. By now he was outside, stumbling around in the dark. "I know you're out here!"

Sean and Melissa crouched low in the shadows, holding their breaths and hoping Jeremiah wouldn't do any more damage.

"I know you're here!"

"He's heading straight for us," Melissa whispered.

Sean nodded. "We better make a run for it."

And then suddenly they heard Mortimer yell, "Ah . . . it's got me!"

BLAM! BLAM! BLAM!

He fired three blasts into the darkness and managed to hit one pane of glass directly over their heads.

K-RASH!
TINKLE! TINKLE! TINKLE!

Melissa screamed, but Mortimer was so busy screaming himself that he didn't hear.

"Help, get it off! Get it off!"

Now Anna was in the yard. "What are you doing?" she shouted. "You shot out the window!"

"It's on my head! Help! Get it off!"

RIBBIT!

"Why, you idiot!" Anna yelled as she grabbed something on his head and flung it to the ground. "It's only a frog!"

"You know how I feel about frogs!" Mortimer whimpered.

"You shot up our house because of a stupid frog?"

"But it was on my head! And it's all dark out here and . . . and . . ."

"It's just a power outage," Anna snapped. "They'll have it back on in a second. Honestly, sometimes . . ."

"I'm sorry," he whimpered, sounding very much like a little boy talking to his mommy.

"Oh . . . it's okay," Anna said. "It's been a long evening. Come on. Let's go to bed. We're going to have a busy day tomorrow."

But, even now as they hid in the shadows, Sean and Melissa were forming a plan.

10

Wrapping Up

SATURDAY, 18:04 PDST

All Saturday afternoon, Sean and Melissa had worked on the plan. And by Saturday night, everyone and everything was ready.

"Okay, does everybody know what they're supposed to do?" Sean asked.

"Check!" Melissa exclaimed. "I'm on my way to Doc's house."

"KC?"

"Check!" She held out a big bag full of slimy green frogs.

RIBBIT . . . RIBBIT . . . RIBBIT . . .

"Spalding?"

"Check! One newsboy at your service!"

"Bear?"

Silence.

"Bear?!"

More silence.

"Bear, wake up!"

"Huh . . . what?"

"Are you ready to put our plan into action?"

"Oh . . . yeah . . . got it right here."

He fished around in his pocket, pulling out two pieces of bubble gum, a slightly used tissue, an assortment of candy bar wrappers, and, finally, one crumpled piece of paper. He straightened it out, slowly read it over, and then stiffly recited . . .

"My job is to wait at the circuit breaker. When you give the signal, I cut the power."

"Great!" Sean said. "And I'll make sure the police are there."

"This is gonna be fun," KC said. "But why didn't you just call the police and let them take care of it?"

"Because it would be our word against Anna and Mortimer's," Sean said. "And in case you haven't noticed, they've become heroes around this town."

"So this way. . . ?"

"This way, the police can catch them red-handed. And, if we do it right, they'll confess to everything."

Melissa turned to Bear. "So, Bear, think you can stay

awake long enough to help us pull this off?"

Bear gave a crisp salute. "You can count on me!"

"Great!" Sean said. "Let's go!"

SATURDAY, 18:45 PDST

"Hey, Chief," the desk sergeant called, "got a kid on the phone who says he has some important information about the vampires."

"Really? What's this make, fifteen calls today?"

"Sixteen."

"Guess I might as well take this one, too."

"Line four."

The chief punched line four. "Chief Robertson."

"Chief, this is Sean Hunter."

"Sean Hunter . . ." The chief was obviously trying to place the name.

"You remember me. Bloodhounds, Incorporated?"

"Bloodhounds, In . . . Oh sure! You and your sister. You're the ones who solved that Invisible Knight case."

"That's right."

"And that UFO thing."

"Yes, sir. Well, I've got some important information about the vampires. I need you to have an unmarked car parked across the street from 814 Myrtle Avenue tonight between 8:30 and 9:45."

The chief laughed. "Listen, son. You and your sister have helped us out a couple of times, that's true. But I've had every man on my force looking for that vampire. What makes you think you can do what twenty-four trained policemen haven't been able to do?"

"Chief, this is real important."

"Okay, okay. Listen. If I can spare a car, I'll send it on over. But I'm not promising."

"But, Chief!"

"Sorry, kid. We're getting lots of calls, and we simply can't respond to all of 'em." With that, he hung up just as the desk sergeant appeared in the doorway, carrying a cup of coffee.

"Who was it, Chief?"

"One of those Bloodhound kids. John . . . Sean . . . Hunter, I think."

"Their dad owns the radio station KRZY."

"You know 'em?"

"Yeah. Good kids. Go to my church."

"Well," the chief sighed, shaking his head, "he has some crazy idea about catching the vampires tonight."

The desk sergeant carried his coffee in and sat down. "I don't know, Chief. If Sean Hunter says he knows something about the vampires, then he knows something about the vampires."

SATURDAY, 19:58 PDST

The kids waited as Anna and Mortimer prepared to leave the house to make their final robbery. The attempt at Bear's house had failed, and they still needed one more.

Spalding was the first to go into action. He ran up to the couple as they stepped out the front door, preparing to head for their limo.

"Uh . . . excuse me. I'm selling subscriptions to the Midvale Daily Sun, and I was wondering if perhaps—"

"Not interested, kid," Mortimer said.

"I certainly appreciate that; however, for a mere twenty-five dollars a week—"

"He said we're not interested," Anna snapped. "Beat it."

"But if I can procure three thousand dollars worth of subscriptions, I will have earned a discount trip to Disneyland—"

"Kid, I told you . . ."

As Spalding continued the distraction, KC sneaked behind them, quietly carrying her bag full of frogs into the house. When he saw that she was safely inside, Spalding quickly dropped the sales pitch. "On second thought," he said, "I've been to Disneyland more times than I can count anyway. Forget it." With that, he turned and strolled away.

"Crazy kid," Mortimer said as he shut the door, locked it, then turned and headed for the limo.

Now inside the house, KC began finding the best possible locations for her frogs. Two of them went onto the sofa. Two more under the table. Three in the closet where Mortimer hung his vampire suit. A couple in the kitchen, one in the bathroom . . . On and on she went, having the time of her life.

Watching from across the street, Melissa sighed, "I wish I could be in there doing that."

"Your time will come, sis," he said. "Just be patient."

The bag was emptied quicker than KC wanted. She exited the front door and joined the others on the street. Now all they had to do was wait for the couple to return.

SATURDAY, 20:38 PDST

Sean watched from across the street as the long black limo turned the corner onto Myrtle Avenue. Through his binoculars he could see Anna and Mortimer laughing as they drove home from their final vampire attack. They had no idea about the little "surprise party" waiting for them.

Sean picked up his walkie-talkie and whispered, "Here they come! Are you ready?"

"Ready," Melissa said as she stood waiting in the

shadows. Domesticus IV was beside her, eagerly awaiting a little housework at 814 Myrtle Avenue.

Anna and Mortimer climbed out of the limo, stretched, and entered the house.

Quickly the kids raced around to the backyard and slowly raised up to look in the window. Inside, Mortimer and Anna sat down at the kitchen table to enjoy a victory glass of champagne and to count their latest money when . . .

RIBBIT!

"Something's on my foot." Mortimer looked under the table and screamed. "A frog! There's a frog on my foot! Get it off! Get it off!"

He jumped up and began a frightened little dance around the room.

"It's just a frog!" Anna yelled. "Calm down!"

RIBBIT! RIBBIT! RIBBIT!

"Aughhh!" Mortimer screamed. "There's hundreds of them! Thousands of them! They're everywhere! Aughhh!"

"Mortimer! Get a grip!"

But he wouldn't get a grip. In fact, Anna had to leap to her feet and slap him across the face to bring him back to his senses. Not a bad idea . . . except it knocked his extrathick glasses off his face.

"Oh no, I'm blind!" he screamed. "They attacked my eyes! The frogs attacked my eyes!"

"Mortimer! You're hysterical!"

RIBBIT! RIBBIT! RIBBIT!

He staggered around the room, bumping into the table, into the wall, and into the . . .

K-RASH!
K-SPLASH!
glug . . . glug . . . glug . . .

. . . giant fish aquarium, which dumped water all over the floor (not to mention a few slimy fish), making Mortimer all the more panicky.

"Augh! Augh! Augh!"

Which only made Anna shout louder. "Mortimer! Morti—WOAH!"

Until she stepped on one of those slippery little critters. Her feet shot out from under her. "EEEE!" and she . . .

K-BAMB!

. . . landed flat on her back. "Groan . . ."

RIBBIT! RIBBIT! RIBBIT!

As she lay there on the wet floor, a frog jumped on top of her head and became tangled in her thick hair. Unfortunately, she was in such pain, she didn't notice. Slowly, painfully she staggered to her feet. "Mortimer, darling." She grabbed his shoulders and pulled his face into her face. "You've got to get a hold of your—"

But that was all she said before Mortimer saw the frog in her hair—an inch from his face. Now he really went berserk!

"AUGHHHHH! A FROG! A FROG!"

"Oh no," Anna moaned. "Now he thinks *I'm* a frog!"

Mortimer picked up a nearby ashtray and threw it at the frog in his wife's hair. She almost ducked in time. Almost. The impact left her a little dazed as she began to stagger around the room. Around the room and straight toward Mortimer!

And without his glasses, all Mortimer could see was the blurry green thing in her hair.

RIBBIT! RIBBIT! RIBBIT!

"STAND BACK!" he shouted. "I'M WARNING YOU!" He picked up a heavy pepper mill from the table and swung it at the frog tangled in her hair.

Fortunately for Anna, she ducked again. Unfortunately, the lid came off the mill, and black pepper flew everywhere!

"Morti . . . AH-CHOO . . . mer! Morti . . . AH-CHOO . . . mer!"

"STAY . . . AH-CHOO . . . BACK. STAY . . . AH-CHOO . . . BACK!"

"It's time!" Sean yelled into his walkie-talkie. "Send him in!"

Melissa looked up at her big metal friend. "Domesticus," she said, "it's time to clean house!"

Mortimer and Anna were still sneezing when Domesticus crashed through the door.

THIS . . . PLACE . . . IS . . . A . . . MESS. I . . . WILL . . . NOW . . . BEGIN . . . CLEANING.

"EAAAGHHH!" Anna screamed.

"IT'S A MONSTER!" Mortimer yelled.

First Domesticus cleaned the table by scooping up all the money and throwing it in the dishwasher.

"HE'S . . . AH-CHOO . . . GOT ALL . . . AH-CHOO . . . OUR MONEY!" Anna cried.

"FROGS!" Mortimer screamed, standing on a chair as they hopped around on the wet floor below.

RIBBIT! RIBBIT! RIBBIT!

"GET THEM AWAY! GET THEM AWAY!"

THIS . . . PLACE . . . IS . . . A . . . MESS. THIS . . . PLACE . . . IS . . . A . . . MESS . . . Domesticus moved faster as he turned on the dishwasher and began pulling dishes from the cabinets, smashing them onto the floor.

"THE MONSTER'S GONE MAD!" Anna screamed.

RIBBIT! RIBBIT! RIBBIT!

"GET THEM AWAY! GET THEM AWAY!"

THISPLACEISAMESS! THISPLACEISAMESS!

Outside, Sean gave the signal to Bear, who cut the power, plunging the house into total darkness.

That was the final straw. Mortimer and Anna ran out the door and into the street, screaming for their lives.

"EEEAAUUGHHHH . . ."

"GET THEM AWAY! GET THEM AWAY!"

Officers West and Smith sat in their patrol car across the street. They were bored and eating doughnuts when they saw Anna and Mortimer running out of their house screaming.

"Look!" Officer Jones pointed to Mortimer, who was still in his vampire suit. "It's a vampire!"

The two policemen scrambled out of their patrol car and raised their badges high in the air.

"Halt!"

"Officers!" Mortimer screamed, gasping for breath. "You've got to help us!"

"Big metal monsters from space!" Anna cried. "They're going to kill us all!"

"And frogs!" Mortimer shrieked. "Frogs are everywhere! Big, green, nasty ones!" He looked back to Anna, saw the frog in her hair, and screamed again.

"Excuse me, pal," Officer Jones shouted over him. "Would you mind telling me what you're doing in this vampire costume?"

"Huh? Oh, this? Well, you see . . . uh . . . uh . . ."

"Would you believe we've been to a costume party?" Anna asked.

"I don't think so," Officer Smith said as he reached into their car and pulled out an artist's sketch of the Midvale Vampire. "I think your buddy here's the one we've been looking for."

"Why, that's . . . that's absurd!" Mortimer cried.

"Is it?" the officer asked. "Well, why don't we take a look in your house just to make sure, shall we?"

Meanwhile, as Mortimer and Anna talked to the officers, Sean and Melissa sneaked back into the house to remove Domesticus.

"Domesticus, where are you?" Melissa whispered.

He wasn't in the living room.

No sign of him in the bathroom.

Or the hall.

"Oh . . . there you are!"

Domesticus IV was in the kitchen, peacefully baking a cake.

"Come on, big guy," Melissa whispered. "The police will be here any minute. We'd better get out of here."

SUNDAY, 09:14 PDST

"Let's go, kids, we're going to be late for church!" Dad stood in the doorway, jingling his car keys.

"Just a minute, Dad," Sean begged. "We want to read the article."

Dad sighed and glanced at his watch. "Two minutes . . . and then we're outa here," he said.

Sean nodded, turned back to the newspaper, and read the headlines: "'Local Kids Expose Vampire Hoax.' " He turned to his sister. "Way to go, Misty!"

"Way to go yourself!" she said as they exchanged high-fives.

Sean shook his head. "I've got to hand it to those two," he said. "They were pretty smart."

"Yeah," Melissa agreed, "but not smart enough."

"But using that remote control bat with the camera in its eyes to scope out their victims' houses . . ."

Melissa nodded. "I have to admit, that was pretty clever. But I still don't understand how—"

"Oh, that was simple," Sean interrupted, already knowing her thoughts. "Whatever the bat saw was relayed back to the video screen in the limo, where Anna was waiting. And then, if it looked safe, she signaled Mortimer to go on in. If it didn't look safe—"

"Like at Bear's house, where she saw us?" Melissa asked.

Sean nodded. "Then she'd call the whole thing off."

"Amazing . . ." Melissa took the article and began to read. Suddenly she cried out, "Oh no!"

"What?" Sean asked. "What's wrong?"

"Look! They called me Rebecca! Rebecca Hummer! They got my name wrong."

Sean shrugged. "Oh well, I guess that's the breaks."

"And they've got your name as Sam."

"WHAT? Give me that!"

Of course, Melissa was right. The newspaper said the "vampires" had been caught by a group of kids, including a Rebecca and Sam Hummer.

"How could they do that?" Sean complained.

"I'm sorry, guys," Dad said as he put his hands on both of their shoulders. "But *I* know who the real heroes are, and I'm very proud of both of them. Besides, you did get that hundred-dollar reward from Mrs. Tubbs."

"Yeah," Sean sighed. "But that won't even begin to pay for all the damage Domesticus did."

"Well, there will be other cases," Dad said. Then, glancing at his watch, he added, "Hey, we better get going."

"Okay," Sean said, "we're coming. Oh, and Dad . . ."

"Yeah?"

"Thanks!"

"For what?"

"For helping us remember that 'The one who is in you is greater than the one who is in the world.' "

Dad smiled. "Try never to forget that."

Sean nodded. "I know." Then, turning to go, he asked, "Are you ready, Rebecca?"

"Ready when you are, Sam!"

With that, all three laughed and headed toward the door. Little did they know that another mystery was already beginning. One that would require all of their cunning, all of their experience, and all of their faith. . . .

By Bill Myers

Children's Series:

Bloodhounds, Inc. — mystery/comedy
Journeys to Fayrah — fantasy/allegorical
McGee and Me! — book and video
The Incredible Worlds of Wally McDoogle — comedy

Teen Series:

Forbidden Doors

Adult Novels:

Blood of Heaven
Threshold

Nonfiction:

Christ B.C.
The Dark Side of the Supernatural World
Hot Topics, Tough Questions

99A